Hook Her for God

Hook Her for God

A hooked for God novel

Tasha Leona

Hook Her for God

Published in Canada by D Vine Publishing 2013

Published in Canada 2013 by D Vine Publishing

Paperback ISBN: 978-0-9919261-0-7

Hook Her for God is dedicated to my Mother, Dorothy Hamilton and the memory of my Father, Carleton Hamilton. Both of my parents have taught me the love of God through their actions and unfailing love.

Acknowledgements

A special thank-you to my Husband Alton, and my five children, Jahmar, Natayjah, Jahtaya, Elijah and Jahnay, for being the best family and support system in the world. Without all of you, I would not be where I am today and I am forever grateful.

I also want to thank the following people who have supported me on my journey of becoming a Published Author. You either took the time to read my raw, unedited manuscript and/or inspired me to be the best I can possibly be. Nadine, Grace, Gabriel, Nicole, Arlene, Pastor Pat Francis and all my family and friends.

And last but not least, I want to give all the praise and glory to Jesus Christ my Lord and Saviour who gave me the idea for this book and sat with me and whispered ideas in my ears and heart during this whole process.

Prologue † Aaron

It is funny. I can remember the first day I stepped into this church as if it were yesterday. I thought it was a joke. It had to be a joke. Everything this church stood for had nothing to do with my life. What would God want with me? What could these people possibly know about me, my life or the hardships I endured? Seriously, why would they care?

Here I was, twenty-one, with a two-year-old daughter who came complete with a deadbeat dad. The only possible way I knew to survive was by lying on my back with disgusting men and forcing myself to think about anything but the act that was taking place. You do not need to judge me—I do an amazing job of judging myself.

Here they were, all dressed to the nines, singing, swaying, clapping and crying. What could these square heads have to cry about? To be fair, their tears were not the same kind of tears I cried. My tears told a story of betrayal, hurt, loss, sadness and fear. Theirs were definitely coming from a different place because, I wondered, how on earth do you cry, smile and sing at the same time? They had to be high on crack, marijuana or something else. That was the only way I knew people to look so satisfied and happy. That was the only way to escape the perils of the world and feel good. Yes, it had to be the drugs.

Oh yeah, by the way, my name is Aaron. Aaron—no middle name—Hope. Everything about my name is ridiculous. To start, my mother was too lazy to think of a middle name. That was all right though because my most entertaining childhood game was based on finding a suitable middle name depending on what I was going through or whom I wanted to be when I grew up. It was fun and kept me occupied for hours.

Secondly, a schoolteacher told me that the meaning of my first name is 'exalted one'. She even told me the story of Aaron who, in the Bible, is Moses' younger brother, and in my opinion, played a secondary role to his older brother. Moses was the chosen one but Aaron did a lot of the work and did not get credit for it. Well, I play a secondary role to no one. You can believe that!

Then there is the matter of my last name. Hope. What a pathetic name. It is not a solid or strong name. It holds no weight or power. Just because you hoped for something, that did not mean you were going to get it.

Looking back at my life, you would not believe the amazing changes that happened, and continue to happen. If I did not live it, I would not believe my story either. I thank God daily for loving and blessing me.

Who knew that I would also come to be a part of this church group and actually belong? Who knew that He could actually love a young, dirty, runaway prostitute and make her as clean and deserving as the rest of the people in this church?

My story definitely mirrors a caterpillar. Imagine crawling along the dirty ground and the rough, jagged trees your entire life, only to be transformed into a beautiful butterfly that soars high above the ground in the peaceful sky. Well, that is the best way to describe what happened to me. Jesus saved my life and changed me but, trust me, getting there was not easy...

One † Aaron

"**H**mm-mm, baby you always know how to make me feel so good! You know how to hook a brother up!" My regular customer with the scar on his lower back stretched his long frame comfortably on my king size bed as though it were his own. We had both just woken up and I was still feeling a bit groggy.

I rolled over from my back to my stomach to look at him and I tried to remember what his name was. OK, I'm lying. I know his name. It is Brandon and apart from the ugly scar on his back, he is perfect! Brandon is one of my only customers that I actually do remember his real name because I love saying it softly in my mind. *Bran-don*, hmm-mm, music to my ears.

He is tall, about six foot three with a lean muscular build, just the way I like it. He is always well dressed in business attire and always smells good unlike some of my other funkier smelling clients.

You see, Brandon is different. He does not talk smack to me and he does not try to grope me or force me to do things I do not enjoy.   When I am with Brandon, I feel special. He is the only customer who actually takes the time to meet my needs and make my body feel good. Sometimes I feel like I should be paying him but that is never going to happen. When I am with him, I forget for just a moment that I am a prostitute. He makes me feel like a regular person.

However, sadly, I am not a normal person. Let's keep it real. I'm a street hoe and have to keep myself from forgetting this fact. I make a point of disconnecting emotionally from my customers. One tactic I use is not calling them by their real names. Instead, I use nicknames. I call Brandon *Scar* for the obvious reason that he has the scar on his lower back.

Brandon gives me the biggest grin and I realize I was staring at him pretty intensely. I look away slightly embarrassed but he grabs my chin and turns my face towards him.

"Girl, I think I'm falling for you...seriously. I feel like this thing we have going on here is real. I feel like our connection is strong and deep." Scar pushed himself up onto his elbows to look directly at me, "Aaron, I think about you all the time.   I wanted to ask you..."

"Ask me what?" I say in a low voice.

Oh no, this cannot be happening!   Damn, Damn, Damn it! He must have picked up my vibe because he is looking at me all sappy and drippy. As much as I like him, I cannot let my guard down; this is exactly what Ruby told me would happen if I did. First desire, then love, and lastly a broken heart. She warns me about this on a regular basis. What do I do? How did this happen? I have to shut this foolishness down.

"Don't even go there Scar!" I shouted at him as I sat up and pulled the sheets wrapping them around me. I made a point to tower over Brandon to intimidate him. I had to get control over this situation before it got completely out of hand.

What was going on here? Damn, looks like Brandon is sprung like all the rest. To think, I was really starting to enjoy his company.

"Yo, get up and leave now!" I barked at him, "and make sure you leave my money on the table!"

Brandon turned and looked at me in shock. His face registered different emotions. He opened his mouth to say something and quickly snapped it shut. After a few seconds, he slowly slid out of the bed naked not breaking eye contact with me.

As I kept my glare strongly focused on him, I could feel bile rise up in my throat but I quickly swallowed it. This was a much unexpected response. Brandon is the only customer who did not have me running out of bed to puke my guts out for five minutes straight after an encounter like everyone else. The sick feeling I have right now is not from disgust though- it is from anxiety. He was not going to win this one, I stared him down like a pit bull ready to attack.

"Remember," I added to get my point across and remind him who was in charge "you spent the whole night so that's extra, my stuff isn't free and this right here" I pointed to my multi-million dollar private area "is not a charity!"

If Brandon thought he was going to drop a few compliments on me like some naive little school girl to get away with not giving me my money, he had another thing coming.

He picked up his clothes at the bottom of my bed and as he was getting dressed, he turned and looked at me with hurt in his eyes that was shortly replaced by another expression. Was that anger or hatred that I saw?

"Whatever Aaron!" he growled.

He placed three extra red bills on the pile of money he was leaving on the small table beside my door. He opened the door to leave but then paused and turned around to face me.

"It's OK baby, you are definitely worth the overtime fee, a hot little sexy number like you," and with a malicious look on his face he added "Hopefully, you raise your little one right so by the time you lose your looks, she can take over your...(cough)...business!"

I could not move or speak as he slowly licked his beautiful lips and blew me a kiss.

"All I was going to ask you for was permission to take a shower. What did you think I was going to say huh? Did you really think I was going to ask you to be my girl or something? Ha! See you on Thursday baby!" and with that he left slamming the door behind him. Shortly after, I heard the front door slam and the clinking of the chain lock as it slammed against the door.

His words ripped through me like a roaring chainsaw. I let the sheet drop to the floor and I sat on my bed naked, numb and in shock. Several minutes passed before I could actually move. It felt like hours before I actually took a breath. In that very moment, I experienced every single emotion that a human being could possibly own. I went from freezing cold to piping hot in record time.

What did he just say to me? That low life piece of garbage had the nerve to mention my little girl. I don't care what he thinks or says about me but he cannot talk about my baby.

I looked over in the direction of her crib grateful to hear her rhythmic breath indicating the noise had not awakened her and she was still asleep.

I got up, tiptoed over to the crib, and looked down at her. She was so precious, beautiful, and innocent, everything that I was not.

This was the first time since her birth that I really thought about her future and her life. I always forced myself not to connect my dirty lifestyle with the one I raised my daughter in but now I wondered if they were the same. I have been fooling myself all along.

Looking around my one bedroom apartment which is located on the top of a store in one of the busiest locations downtown; I no longer felt good about my surroundings. Normally, I am so content with my habitat. My apartment is one of the best looking in a sought out location thanks to my flair for home decorating, keen eye and oodles of money I make. It's a great size and I get compliments on it all the time. I do not want to sound arrogant but my place is definitely something to brag about and normally feels comfortable and warm. But today the walls of the apartment appear as though they were closing in and suffocating me. It felt filthy, nasty, and cheap. Just like how I feel inside.

My baby girl cannot turn out like me, I thought as I grabbed my favourite nightshirt off the red suede ottoman and pulled it on to cover my shame. I cannot, no; I will not ever allow her to live this kind of life!

So all this time Brandon thinks I am a no good piece of meat right?   What did he think; I would raise my daughter to take my place once I got older and lost my touch?

Boiling hot tears starting rolling from my eyes and splashed my cheeks. I wiped away my tears and runny nose with my shirtsleeve.

"I can't get soft," I stated, angry that I had allowed myself to cry "this world will eat me and my baby alive if I do. No, no, no! My period must be coming to make me feel so emotional." I said aloud because I had to justify my tears.

I desperately needed a cup of coffee to help me refocus and gain my composure. Today's coffee would be black. None of the cream and sugar I usually used, I needed it to be brutal and bitter- just like Brandon.

I headed towards the kitchen, focusing on my steamy cup of goodness. Then it happened. *The voice.* The damn voice that I have heard in my head since I can remember came back.

"Aaron, this is not the life I have for you, I have so much more to offer" I heard in my mind.

"Quiet!" I screamed out loud and covered my ears as I sank down to the ground. I listened and I heard nothing more. As quickly as the voice came it left. I waited a moment to make sure it was gone before I slowly collected myself up off the ground.

Great, on top of everything else I experienced this morning, the voice had to return. When will it ever go away for good? The voice came more frequently since I left home and went to live on the streets. I dare not tell anyone about it because only crazy people hear voices and I know I am not crazy. It is not a scary voice, just an annoying one. It's as though my conscience developed an audible voice and visits me in desperate times of need. I could not focus on the voice right now; it was the least of my worries.

I knew things needed to change. No, let me rephrase that, they had to change. If I did not choose to change for me, then I had to for her. My precious little baby girl Angel. She is the only person in the world that truly matters to me. The only person I will ever love. For the first time in a long time, I was afraid.

"It's not only about me anymore." I whispered to myself as I slinked off into my washroom to shower and wash the stench of that parasite Scar off me, "things have to change."

I turned the pipe on and made the water as hot as I could possibly take and immersed myself into the blades of my punisher. The water seemed to boil me alive but I could handle it. This was routine punishment I inflicted on myself for being a whore. It was a ritual I used to try to wash off the filth of my very existence. As I braced myself against the stinging pain, I let it serve as a reminder to me of the eternal heat I would feel after I left this earth and burned in hell. At least that is what that Christian woman who frequently patrolled the prostitution strip shouted at me whenever she passed me.

"I hate Scar, I absolutely hate him!" I screamed in the shower as figments of his verbal attack replayed repeatedly in my mind.

As I rested my forehead against the tiled shower wall, I knew deep down inside it was not really him I hated. I hated myself. I hated my life. I hated the hand in life that I had been dealt. I mean, he had a right to a rebuttal; I said some harsh things to him but it hurt that he said something so insensitive about my child.

As the tears streamed down my cheeks yet again, they were easier for me to ignore this time as they blended into the drops of water cascading down from my shower faucet that I had pre-set to the raindrop feature. In here, nobody will ever see or hear my pain. No one will know how vulnerable I really am.

Two † Brandon

Brandon wondered what was playing on the radio as he turned it on.

"What is this? Gaga?" he scoffed out loud then laughed as he remembered her full stage name was Lady Gaga.

Where were the real women and the real music of yesterday? Nobody knew anything about music now. Gone were the days when you could hear musicians like SWV, En Vogue or Patti LaBelle on the airwaves. These singers were worthy of being called ladies.

Brandon turned off the music and focused on his early morning drive home, as the sun played on the windshield. Truthfully, he preferred thinking about her—his sweet, beautiful Aaron—in silence anyway. July was proving to be on schedule with the suffocating heat of summer and although it was still early, he felt his car heating up. He rolled down the window, hoping that the summer breeze would trump his need to turn on his air conditioner. He preferred natural resources to manufactured devices.

As Brandon slowed his car to obey the upcoming traffic lights that had just turned yellow, he reflected on the battle he just had with Aaron in her apartment. What happened in there? None of it made sense. He had finally worked up the courage to tell her how he felt about her. It seemed like such a perfect moment. For the first time since he started hooking up with her, she actually did not kick him out and fell asleep in his arms. It took him a long time to fall asleep because he felt so content as he stared down into her beautiful face. Without makeup and her slinky clothing, she looked as innocent as an angel. He was overjoyed and compassionate as he held her, thinking that they would be good together.

Earlier on, she had let him hold and feed her beautiful daughter. He was caught off guard and jumped at the opportunity. Her daughter, Angel, was a darling little girl and reminded him that the children he longed to have were for now just a fantasy.

It was not just about sex. It felt like so much more. She actually relaxed around him, and for a moment he felt like he was her man and they were a family. Well, he was so wrong. What was the term he heard those young teenage boys say the other day? Oh, yeah. "Epic fail." This was definitely an epic fail.

As he drove home along Yonge Street, barely taking in all the changes that had been made to the downtown area of Toronto in the past year or two, he let his mind drift back to the first day he met her...

Brandon had left Toronto's downtown mall, the Eaton Centre, that day feeling sad and happy at the same time. He was on a lunch break when he got the call that his divorce from his wife of six months was finalized. The sadness came from a place of failure and resentment for the time he and his now ex, Tanika, shared and wasted together. The happiness came from the feeling of freedom, and being able to finally move on and live his life.

To be fair, the relationship with Tanika was not always bad. In the beginning, it was unbelievably good. Everyone who knew them labelled them the perfect couple.

He was introduced to her at his friend Dimitri's birthday party and they just clicked. They had both graduated from the University of Toronto, had successful careers in finance and were looking for love.

At the young age of twenty, Brandon was ready to settle down with a hard working woman with whom he could build a strong family life.

Tanika fit the bill to the letter—at least that was what he thought. Even his hard-to-please lawyer father gave Brandon his approval. After all, she was not a moocher who only wanted him as a *baby daddy* so she could take his money, as his father had described any woman Brandon had met after he graduated.

She had a solid career, drove one of the baddest BMWs on the block and had a savings account that would please any man. She was charming and funny, and all his friends enjoyed her company because she could hang with the boys. As Tanika's true colours began to surface, it did not take long for him to learn that these qualities were a curse, not a blessing.

They had made the mistake of not talking about their future goals, the lives they wanted and family values. Brandon dreamed of having at least two children and welcomed the idea of more. He longed to settle down and build the family bond he was robbed of in his childhood. He had a scar on his lower back as a reminder of this loss. He wanted to be everything his father was not.

Tanika on the other hand, viewed the idea of children negatively. Children would cause her hips and butt to spread and stop her from travelling the world anytime she wanted. To her, they represented nothing but a loss of looks and freedom.

No amount of charm or money was a solution for the endless arguments they had. Tanika grew to resent him and it was not long before she crossed the line. Rumours were quickly spreading that Tanika slept with one of Brandon's friends and when he confronted her, she admitted to the act as if it was nothing.

"Live a little, baby," she said. "We're too young to act like an old married couple. At the end of the day, it's you I'm coming home to. Isn't that enough?"

The memory of those words sent chills up and down Brandon's spine. He packed his bags that very day and never turned back. She did not even come after him and he was not surprised. He knew that both of them were relieved to end their loveless relationship.

The news of his divorce was cause for celebration. It was not long and drawn out like other divorces he had heard of. He bought her out and got to keep the house, which pleased him. Tanika never liked it anyways. She wanted to live in a cold, concrete condominium, preferring a minimalist, modern style of living. Brandon had insisted on buying a house and would not bend when it came to what he wanted. He had a big family in mind and would not give up on his goals and ambitions. She was not thrilled, but had given in.

After calling his assistant and asking her to take messages because he would be working from home for the rest of the day, he headed off in search of a place to relax. The one thing he liked about downtown Toronto was that there were so many bars and lounges within walking distance of any location. Forget walking, he felt like skipping all the way to the closest venue. He walked aimlessly with no target location in mind. He was focused on the feeling of inner peace he felt inside.

"Hey, sexy businessman. What are you so happy about?" he heard a female voice say.

He turned in the direction of her voice and there she was—his Aaron—standing there, looking so beautiful and sexy.

"Pardon me?" he asked, knowing exactly what she said but was stalling.

He had to talk to this goddess. She looked like she walked off the cover of "Vibe" magazine. She was approximately five foot eight and perfectly proportioned—just the way he liked his women. She had beautiful big brown eyes that seemed to mirror his reflection, the cutest nose and a gorgeous smile. Her hair was curly and black, and she wore it in a daring style. The high-end labels she wore were familiar to him because of Tanika, but she had a way of putting them together that said, "I am unique. I am my own person". The classic Gucci watch on her wrist told him she definitely was not hurting for money.

"You're walking and grinning like the damn Cheshire cat." she said. "What, did you close a big deal or something?"

"You could say that." He chuckled, thinking that is all Tanika ever was—a big deal or something. "You can definitely say that!"

"Want to celebrate?" she asked sashaying towards him with slow, controlled steps. "I'm Aaron and I love sexy men in suits. I'm not cheap but I'm well worth the money."

"Huh?" Brandon was confused.

Her little monologue made her sound like a prostitute but she did not look like the ones you saw working the prostitution strip.

"Come again?"

"I said, 'Do. You. Want. To. Ce-le-brate?'" she repeated slowly, enunciating every syllable. "I'd love to celebrate with you for a price."

"Are you serious?" asked Brandon taking two steps backwards.

Never in his life had Brandon hired a hooker. It did not even cross his mind when he was in university and many of his friends did it. Not only did he find it risky with all the diseases that were spreading from person to person, he also found the idea of hiring someone for sex a big hard blow to his ego. After all, Brandon was quite the catch and never had any problems with getting women. Seriously, if he needed sex, all he had to do was consult the phone book in his old BlackBerry and flip through random numbers. No way, no how would Brandon pay for sex. He could not believe this vision of loveliness was a hooker.

"What's the matter, baby? Are you a virgin?" she laughed. "You afraid to pay for something you can get for free? I already told you, I am worth the money."

"No thanks," he said, shaking his head. "I'm good!"

Brandon had a big problem though. His head was telling him to leave immediately but his feet would not move. How could he? He had never been so captivated by a woman in his entire life. He could sense something special about her, something he did not even find in Tanika. It sounded and felt like crazy talk but he could not walk away.

"Look, I'm not in need of your...," he cleared his throat, "service. But if you'd like, you can join me for a drink and if you're hungry, I'll buy you something to eat." He flashed what he knew was one of his most charming smiles, where his dimples sunk deep into his cheeks and his eyes sparkled. This was the signature lady charmer move that he mastered in high school. He was famous -in his own right- for it.

Aaron cocked her head to one side and sized him up. As she slowly looked him up and down, a smile started to spread across her face.

"Sure, baby, I'll join you," she said, not hiding the look of victory. "But trust me, dinner will not be the only thing you pay for tonight!" With that, she forced her arm through his and led him towards a bar.

Aaron was right about two things that day. The first was that he would be paying for more than dinner and the second was she was worth the money. The only thing she failed to mention was that he would fall hard for her. This was the beginning of their very intense, intimate relationship.

Brandon had vowed to win her heart and change her life. He believed love, well, real love, could change a person. He had enjoyed the movie *Pretty Woman* and deemed anything was possible. She could be his Vivian and he could be her Edward.

The problem was this was the most serious businesswoman he ever met. There was no way she would see him without being paid—bottom line. Brandon devised a scheme to win her over, mind, body, soul and heart. He would meet her three times a week under the false pretense of wanting to buy sex from her, but he would look at it as taking care of his woman. He would figure this girl out and make her his lady. There was no girl in the world that could resist his charm. He had been training for this day his entire life.

As Brandon reflected on the first time he saw her, he felt regret in his heart like no other. She really hurt him this morning. What he said about her daughter was careless and stupid, but he only wanted to shut her up and that was the only thing that came to him in the moment. He wished he could take it all back.

As Brandon pulled onto his driveway and parked, he was overcome with grief. He could not move and lowered his head onto the wheel and sighed.

"What have I done?" he said to himself. "I ruined everything. What am I going to do if she refuses to see me again? How do I take back what I said to her?"

Brandon felt tears fall down his cheeks. He did not have the strength or the desire to wipe them away. "No woman, not even Tanika, could make me shed a tear. But here I am crying over a prostitute. What have I got myself into? Who the hell am I?" he cried.

It had been a whole year since he first met Aaron and everything was over in the blink of an eye. In less than two years, Brandon managed to lose a wife and now a woman he had grown to truly love.

Three † Aaron

Well, as they say, there is nothing like retail therapy! I decided that I am not going to let Brandon ruin the rest of my week. I am over him.

To think, two days ago I was so upset by the argument with Brandon that I actually cancelled on two customers. I felt like I suffered a loss and broke up with my boyfriend. What was this world coming to? He was never my man to begin with, only a stupid customer. But I never felt this kind of sadness over any other man in my life except my father—not even my worthless baby daddy, O'Neil.

O'Neil was a wannabe gangster I met on the block with Ruby. There was never any love in our connection but he was slick with his words and good company in bed. He knew what I did professionally and it did not bother him. This was normal in our world. We both hustled. He sold drugs and I sold my body. I made much more money than he did and I knew that sometimes he stole from me. It made me feel powerful knowing that he looked at the things I had with a jealous eye.

O'Neil was careless when it came to wearing protection and because of this, I got pregnant. I was excited but that jerk was pissed off and told me to "get rid of it", as if our baby was something that had no value. When he finally realized I was not going to have an abortion, he started telling people on the block that my baby was not his and that I probably got pregnant with one of my customers. I did not care. I locked him out of my life and moved on, as if it was nothing.

So why was I pining away over Brandon? Oh, heck no, it was time to heal. I feel so good as I walk through the mall looking at the hot new trends in the store windows. I cannot help but feel good that I can afford to walk into any store and buy anything I want.

When I first ran away, I was lucky to have the three outfits in the backpack that I always kept packed and hidden away in case of emergencies. Emergencies just like that night. Shopping in stores like the ones in this mall used to be way out of my league until I met Ruby. Ruby changed my world.

I am jolted out of my thoughts by the soothing vibration of the newest BlackBerry out, buzzing on my hip.

"What's up, girl?" I squeal after checking the phone and seeing Ruby's number. "I was just thinking about you!"

"Meet me at Eaton Centre, beyotch. I saw some sexy boots in Capezio that I want to get for tonight." Ruby says without even returning my greeting.

"I'm already here, beyotch," I laugh heartily. "How long until you get here?"

"I'll be there in ten. Meet me at *the spot*." The line goes dead.

I chuckle. That girl has no manners and never says "bye". I am not offended though, that is just Ruby. She says what she wants and then the conversation is over. Period.

I walk towards *the spot*, a window table at our favourite McDonald's on the second floor of the Eaton Centre. To block out any thoughts of Brandon, I let my mind wander back to the day I met Ruby.

It was just a few weeks since I ran away from home and I was sifting through the dump in the back of a plaza hoping to hit another jackpot. The week prior, I saw the storeowner actually throw out perfectly good clothes because they had minor defects. They were a welcome addition to my meager wardrobe and I was digging through the trash again when I felt the presence of somebody behind me. I turned around and saw her looking at me—a Caucasian girl who, at around five foot three, was shorter than I was, and thick. She was both top and bottom heavy. I had never seen a white girl with that kind of booty before. Her platinum blonde hair was shaved on one side and bobbed on the other. Her eyes were the brightest blue I had ever seen and they seemed out of place with her tough appearance. She was a really pretty woman and she looked older than me, but not by much. I could tell this girl was probably looking for trouble.

"What'cha doin'?" she asked in a demanding tone as she popped a stick of gum into her mouth.

I started salivating at the thought of chewing a fresh piece of gum.

"What's it to you?" I snapped a little too quickly, embarrassed that I was caught rummaging through the garbage.

In that moment, I wished I had better control over my big mouth and fast tongue.

"It really isn't nothing to me but let me explain something to you, little miss. I run this block and anything that goes on here is my business," Ruby said. "So, again, I'm asking you: What. Are. You. Doing?"

Even though it had only been a few weeks, I had lived on the streets long enough to recognize when someone was serious and not to be messed with.

"I'm looking for clothes," I said. "Sometimes these stores actually throw out brand new clothes." Then I humbled myself and whispered in embarrassment, "And once in a while...good food."

Ruby later told me that her heart softened a bit for me, the little scavenger, especially when I mentioned the food. Ruby also never forgot what it was like to actually be hungry—something the majority of the world has no clue about. I reminded Ruby of herself when she found herself homeless and living on the streets. Street life was not easy. It was both dangerous and risky. Anything could happen to you at less than a moment's notice.

I wondered what Ruby was thinking as a black cat walked up to her and started rubbing itself on her leg.

"Where you from?" asked Ruby as she bent down to scoop up the pathetic looking cat. "Where is your family at?"

"Screw my family," I said a little too aggressively. "I'm on my own, surviving day to day. My family members are all dead to me!"

Ruby looked me over for a few minutes as she pet the cat and by the look on her face, seemed to have made a firm decision.

"Come with me, little ones," she said addressing the stray cat and me. "They call me Ruby here on the streets, and I'm gonna take care of you, baby girl. You should be on your knees thanking the universe or something that I found you. I'm gonna show you the best family you'll ever have—street family!" The cat meowed right on time as if it was wondering whether it too was part of the street family. "Yes, kitty, I have a home for the both of you. Today is your lucky day as well." Ruby said.

Who knew that when she left her home that day, Ruby would return with two black strays? Life was full of surprises.

That was the beginning of a better life for me. I had Ruby to thank for my survival. Ruby taught me to hustle the streets and to use my body and make serious money. She eventually helped me to find a place and remained at my side during my turbulent, unexpected pregnancy and childbirth. She taught me how to live like a celebrity, the true meaning of being tough and the true meaning of family. My life revolved around Ruby and Angel, and they were all the family I would ever need.

I order a Big Mac combo for myself and Ruby's favourite, a Double Big Mac combo. Seconds after sitting down at our spot, I smell Ruby's favourite perfume, Dolce & Gabbana Blue, as she slides into the seat across from me.

"So, where you been, girl? How come you haven't answered my calls?" she demands, leaning across the table to show me she is not impressed and means business.

Dressed in black skinny jeans and a black tank top accessorized with a huge skull medallion encrusted with flecks of faux crystals, her look is sexy and intimidating at the same time. I am grateful she is my friend.

"I was home, tripping." I reply without thinking. "I felt a little bummed, so I turned off my phone and stayed inside to clear my head."

"What did you just say to me? Home? Tripping? Girl, what did I teach you?" Ruby asks. "You can't make money by staying inside and not answering your phone. Money is out there on the streets, and you don't have time to be 'home, tripping'. You need to get dem papers!"

I look out the window at the people walking along the busy Queen Street—businessmen, women in suits and sneakers or suits and stilettos, teenagers, lawyers, kids and other hoes. I wish I were down there right now, instead of here with Ruby being cross-examined.

I turn to face Ruby and take a deep breath, knowing what I am about to tell her probably will not be well received.

"The truth is, I've been doing some heavy thinking and I don't know how long I can do this. Things need to change, Rubes. I mean, I need to better myself for Angel," I quicken my words as I notice the annoyed expression that is spreading across Ruby's face. "One day, Angel is going to grow up and I can't let her think that this life is good. I need to better myself for her, so she will want better for herself. The thought of her growing up and living this life makes me wanna..."

"Whoa, princess, slow your roll," Ruby snaps. "Where is this big speech coming from all of a sudden? Is your period here or did you fall down and hit your head? Don't get all Dr. Phil on me. First of all, Angel is only two years old so you have plenty of time to hustle before she gets to an age where it could actually affect her. Second, you are talking crap in my ears. When did you become a Mother Teresa?"

In spite of my inner fear, I chuckle at Ruby's reference to Mother Teresa. In her world and mind, there are only two kinds of women: street hustlers or Mother Teresas—nothing more, nothing less. Street hustlers are those females who had to work their tails off somehow to make money and survive. You know, hookers, drug dealers, pimps and lawyers. The Mother Teresas (everybody else) are women who figured out how to make their money work for them.

"Ruby, I'm not trying to be a Mother Teresa. I just want better for my little girl. I know you feel the same way because I know you love her as much as I do."

Ruby's face softens as she contemplates what I said. One thing I am sure of is that Ruby has a soft spot for Angel. Reminding her of her love for Angel is my only chance to get her to see things my way.

"I guess you're right," she says. "I do want better for our Angel but why you gotta bring this ish up now? It came out of nowhere. What happened to set you off?"

I look out the window again but this time I do not turn back to face her, feeling ashamed of what I am going to tell her.

"Remember Scar, my regular custy? Well, we kinda had a situation and it upset me. We exchanged some harsh words and I guess, well, some of the things he said kinda hurt. Real talk. I've been feeling depressed ever since."

"Oh, no, you didn't!" shouts Ruby.

She reaches across the table and grabs my face to force me to look at her. A couple of people look over at us but she does not care.

"What the heck have I taught you, huh? You getting soft on me? What is my number one rule in this damn game?" she snarls.

I knew it. I should have kept my big mouth shut. I backed myself into this corner and an angry pit bull is guarding the only way out. I have to be strategic about my answer or there are going to be repercussions. Ruby has been lenient with me since she took me under her wing, but I have seen with my own eyes how she deals with her hoes that piss her off. I certainly did not need black and blue added on top of the broken heart I already suffered.

"Not to fall in love with any pricks with sticks!" I answer quickly, before slyly adding, "Or any Joes with Bows."

At the mention of Joes with Bows, Ruby lets go of my face and starts laughing. The inside joke always cheers her up. There is this one square guy who asked Ruby to marry him a few months ago. Squares are Average Joes who work hard for a living and kept their hands clean. This particular guy is named Joe, always wears bow ties and is madly in love with Ruby. The more she disses him, the harder he tries. Secretly, I think she likes him but does not want to admit it. I see how her face lights up when she sees him, even though she pretends not to care.

Thankfully, my approach works and instantly the atmosphere lightens. Ruby sits back and reaches for her burger.

"You know what, Ruby?"

"What?" she replies as she bites into her Double Big Mac.

Where the heck does she store all that food in her five foot three frame?

"I am buying me something blingy today! Screw men! We can buy anything we want for ourselves. The world is ours. Who needs them?" I ask as I raise my McDonald's cup, waiting for her to do the same.

As we toast, I make a mental note: Get a hold of yourself, Aaron. You are slipping. You may have calmed the pit bull down this time but it may rip you to shreds the next time. I need to get over Brandon or Scar or whatever his name is. He is not worth it.

We both finish our meals and get up. It was time to drop some papers and buy some bling. As I said, retail therapy is the answer to everything!

Four † Brandon

Retail therapy is the answer to everything, Brandon thought, as he looked at all the new watches displayed in his favourite jewellery store. There was something about bling that made him feel good.

As a young boy, he had noticed the way his dad's big shot friends sat up and took notice whenever he wore a suit and a new watch. It was almost like the two commodities were the equation for power and respect. The only problem was, it was not power and respect Brandon was after right now—it was something to mend his broken heart.

"Aaron is not worth it! She is not worth it!" Brandon muttered to himself for probably the hundredth time that day.

This very phrase had been his chant for the last couple of days as he tried to convince himself of this truth. Everything had been off since he last saw her. His game was off on the basketball court, where he normally played like a celebrity athlete, and at work, he was sloppy and unfocused. Thankfully, he had an assistant with a keen eye who was able to point out and correct errors before they turned disastrous. At home, he threw nothing but pity parties for himself while throwing back rum and Cokes. He could not get this girl out of his mind and decided to buy a new watch to cheer himself up. That always seemed to work in the past. It was weird how comforting selecting new watches was to him when he was married and going through trauma with Tanika.

Tomorrow was Thursday, the day he normally met up with Aaron at his favourite nightclub. He was worried about her not showing up at all but his mind was set. He was going to go and stay at the club all night if he had to, with fingers crossed, that she would join him.

He had regular scheduled dates with Aaron on Mondays, Thursdays and Saturdays. These were the only days she made available for him. He would have scheduled her in from Monday to Sunday if he could, but she did not keep her money in one pocket. It was the good old "eggs in one basket" philosophy. The thought of her with other men still upset him but he was getting used to it. Thinking about it used to make him so angry that the emotions would stir up in the pit of his stomach and make him sick. He learned to control that feeling and was becoming a pro. Brandon selected a nice watch with a steep price tag and paid for it. He had four suits in mind that this watch would complement.

Just as he was about to leave the store, Brandon saw Aaron heading in his direction with her tough looking friend. He quickly walked to the back of the store and pretended to be interested in the showcase full of cuff links and money clips. Thank goodness he was dressed in his street clothes today. She was used to seeing him in designer suits and hopefully would not recognize him. He pulled his baseball cap low on his forehead, and put up the hood of his hoodie and sunglasses. He knew he must look ridiculous but he was not in the mood for round two of their argument, the cold shoulder or something even worse. He also did not feel comfortable around Aaron's friend, who served as her bodyguard. He could not bear to have the both of them roll up on him right now.

She looked beautiful as usual in a teal blue, fitted halter dress with cute open toe sandals. Her hair was swept over one shoulder, which accented her gorgeous neckline and strong collarbone. Aaron was a total contrast to her friend who wore a full black outfit with a skull medallion hanging slightly below her breasts. She was not an unattractive woman at all; she just had a daunting demeanour. Her piercing blue eyes were beautiful but did not distract from the sharpness in her face.

He could imagine his lips on Aaron's soft smooth neck as he secretly watched her. Instantly, a feeling of longing swept over him. He considered walking up to her and apologizing but he did not want to make their situation any worse. He knew from experience that women were easier to talk to when they were alone, so he decided to play it safe.

"Ruby, let me show you the ring I was telling you about," she said to her friend as she leaned over the glass showcase. "See that one, right there? That's the one!" The two women awed in delight as they admired the ring.

"See, girl, one day my Prince Charming will go down on one knee and ask me to marry him, and this is the ring he is going to give me!" she sighed wistfully.

With a smile, the sales representative retrieved the ring for Aaron to try on. She placed it on her right hand.

"I don't dare jinx it by putting it on my wedding finger. I'm too superstitious so I'll wait for my future husband to do it," she said as she held her hand up in the air and admired it.

"Girl, please," her friend said, rolling her eyes. "You know the rules of this game. If you want this ring, either you or I will have to buy it for you! You know Prince Charming only exists while you are sleeping, roaming about in your dreams, giving you false hope. You know as well as I do that the pimps on the streets will buy it for you in exchange for taking your money and giving you black eyes!"

Aaron instantly lowered her hand, removed the ring and gave it back to the sales associate. Brandon could tell she was not happy.

"Ruby, do you have to ruin everything with your negativity? Am I not even allowed to enjoy my fantasies without you stomping all over them?" she asked, clearly annoyed.

"Hey, I'm just keeping it real, girl. Sorry for interrupting your fantasies or should I call them fake-assies?" Ruby laughed loudly and then walked to another counter to look at earrings and studs.

Aaron remained behind for a minute. Brandon could see the longing in her body language as she gazed at the ring that was now nestled back in the showcase. He also sensed the longing for her fantasy to become a reality. For the first time since meeting her, Brandon saw a vulnerable, soft side in Aaron that he did not know existed.

"Hey, princess, you ready?" her friend asked, jolting Aaron out of her dreams.

Instantly, the vulnerable look on her face was replaced with the hard edge expression he was used to. She squared her shoulders and jutted out her chin.

"Yeah, girl, let's go!" she said in a phony cheerful voice as they left the store.

Brandon couldn't shake that look she had on her face out of his head. He wanted to protect that vulnerable woman inside of Aaron that he had just observed. He wanted to make all her dreams a reality. In that moment he promised himself, yet again, that he was going to do everything he had to do to make it happen. He knew it would be the hardest thing he ever had to do and it would not be easy. For starters, he had to gain her trust again and then he had to make her fall in love with him. He had to be the one to show her that she was much more than a prostitute. He had to change the reflection she saw in the mirror. Brandon approached the sales associate who had been helping Aaron.

"Hello, sir, may I help you with something else?" she asked

"You sure can. That ring that young lady was looking at, can I please see it?"

"No problem," she said taking it out of the display case. "As you probably know, we try to keep our rings unique by only sending a few of each design to each region. This is the only one of its kind here in Ontario."

This was good news.

"I'm planning on asking my girlfriend to marry me soon and this ring is exactly her style. I need you to tell me the truth, do you think it will be here for a while?" he asked

"Between you and me, I don't think so. That young woman who was looking at it, I think she wants to buy it. She has been in here a few times to try it on. So if you really want it, you better buy it quickly," she said.

Brandon knew that she was applying her sales person pressure so she could make a nice commission but he continued to play along. Actually, she gave him the confirmation he needed to do what he was about to do.

"You know what? My girlfriend is special, and I don't want to have any regrets about not buying this ring and having to search for another one. I'll take it," he said.

"Very good, sir. Your girlfriend is a lucky lady," she said before scooping it up and heading towards the cash register.

"Indeed, she is," Brandon said to no one in particular as he followed the sales associate.

Brandon left the store feeling a lot better and much more confident than he had when he entered it. Bubbles of expectation erupted in his belly at the thought of what he hoped was to come. He was cultivating a plan that showed him a promising future. He had to look at Aaron as a challenge and everyone who knew Brandon, knew he lived for challenges. They fueled him. This mission would be even more difficult than winning respect from his father. He smiled, as he thought about the wonderful reward he would get if he were successful.

Brandon quick-stepped it out of the mall and headed in the direction of the elevators, which would take him up to the covered parking area. He was so thankful that he decided to go shopping today. Fate wanted them to be together, it was obvious. He happened to be at the right place at the right time, and he fully intended to take advantage of that fact.

Five † Aaron and Angel

"Just in time," I say as I shut off my favourite home decorating show on HGTV and get up off the couch. I head over to the crib where minutes ago my Angel was sleeping but is now standing up, holding onto the side of the crib.

"Hey, precious baby. How's my little girl?" I ask Angel in a cutesy voice as I pick her up and plant a kiss on her tender cheek.

Now that my little girl is getting older, her sleeping schedule is regulated and it gives me enough time to take in my shows while she naps.

Even after two years, I still cannot get over the fact that Angel is all mine. She is absolutely darling. I study her face for the millionth time;

taking in every detail I already know so well—her button nose, chubby cheeks, thick eyelashes and pretty lips.

For the umpteenth time today, I think about her future. My dreams and aspirations for her are so high and I know that as her mother, I have to give her all the things I did not get. She is undoubtedly the absolute love of my life. I have to be a better mother to Angel than the one who gave birth to me. The phone vibrates, interrupting my thoughts, and I answer it.

"Hey, Aaron, me again," says a small but bubbly voice on the other end.

It is Carmen, Carm for short. She is a nice eighteen-year-old girl, who I met at the park and hired to be Angel's baby-sitter. Angel absolutely adores her.

"Have you decided what you want to do? I want to know if I should make other plans or not," she says.

Today is Thursday and I normally meet Brandon at the club for a full night of fun but we have had absolutely no contact since our argument and I am not sure if I want to see him. I have replayed the whole scene in my mind over and over. If I am going to be honest with myself, I reacted badly when Brandon was a tad bit too affectionate towards me. He was probably still on cloud nine from the amazing night of pleasure and fun we had. His loving words scared me and I am not one hundred percent sure why. He was not the first customer who went gaga over me but he gave me this weird feeling when he said it. It was a feeling I did not recognize and I did not know how to react.

Okay, again, I am not being completely honest. I kind of know why it bothered me. I am starting to "feel" him. There is definitely something different about Brandon.

When I am meeting him, I actually have a nervous, giddy feeling. I find myself taking extra time and care in my appearance and feel tingly everywhere—yup, even down there! I feel so out of control when I am with him.

I was not going to bother meeting him today, especially after what he said about Angel but something inside of me does not like that decision. I know I should be mad at him but I want to believe he only said what he did because he was upset. I am pretty sure he was embarrassed. Look at the way I shut him down. One thing I learned about most men is that you have to be sensitive to their pride.

"You know what, Carm? Come over at the regular time. I'm going to go out after all," I tell her.

Regardless of how I feel, Brandon pays me. If nothing else, it is a business partnership.

"Alright, girl, I'll see you at seven. Bye."

"Bye, see you soon," I reply and end the call.

I refocus my attention on my little girl who is now sitting on the floor and playing with her toys.

"Mama!" she squeals as she stretches her hands out towards me, twinkling her fingers for me to pick her up. I sit down and pull her into my lap for a big squeeze.

"You want some yummy grape juice, baby?" I ask as I point to her Dora sippy cup.

"Juuuusss," she echoes as she tries to pronounce the word and nods her head.

"Dora, Dora, Dora!" she claps her tiny hands in excitement.

She absolutely loves *Dora the Explorer* and I have made sure to build a collection of her favourite character in anything possible—Dora shoes, dresses, pillows. You name it, she has it. Ruby wanted me to deck her out in designer brands. But having loved Barbie as a child and only getting a second-hand doll with chewed up hair and pen marks all over her face, which I cherish even now; I have vowed that my baby would get the desires of her heart. And her desire right now is Dora. I sit Angel in her Dora plush chair and give her the cup then sit down in my banana yellow wing chair and watch her drink. After turning on her favorite DVD, I am alone with my thoughts for a while and allow my mind to drift back to Brandon.

I am actually nervous about going to see him tonight and even more skittish than usual. What if he is rude to me? What if he continues to speak to me in that awful tone of voice he used the last time? What if he does not show up? Worst of all, why do I care? Damn. That weird feeling is rising in my stomach again. I cannot even tell Ruby or anyone how I feel. I have to keep all of this madness bottled up inside. I swear I am going to spontaneously combust!

I barely want to admit this to myself and I dared not tell Ruby, but when we were looking at the ring, I envisioned Brandon as the person giving it to me. It was a stupid fantasy because everyone knows you cannot turn a customer into your life partner, especially in my line of work. But if I believe this then I have to believe that I can never be a wife. All these thoughts have me feeling as if I have lost control of my life.

Damn, this is my time with Angel. I should not be thinking about Brandon. This is another rule I have, not mixing my business life with my personal life. But here I am, thinking about him. I quickly get up, go sit on the floor beside Angel's chair and draw her closer to me to distract my mind from thoughts of Brandon. This is much better. There is nothing like a toddler's TV show to snap your mind back to where it is supposed to be.

"Ma-ma," Angel says half-heartedly as she feels me move closer to her, without taking her eyes off the television.

"You watching *Sesame Street*, baby girl?" I ask her with a grin.

She giggles as Cookie Monster sings C is for cookie and then sloppily gobbles up the cookie.

"Cooookie," she says shaking her cup up and down in delight. "I want cookie!"

My eyes dart to the ash blonde hardwood floor I had professionally installed a while ago to see if any juice managed to grace it. No juice, but I notice something sticking out from underneath the chocolate brown loveseat.

"Hmm, what's this?" I ask.

I pick up a picture Brandon and I took on a whim at one of those photo booths in the mall. There are four pictures and we struck weird, goofy poses in each one. Distracted by the picture, I do not notice Angel standing over me, pointing to the picture and smiling.

"Dada," she squeals and claps her hands.

Huh? Dada? Where on earth did she learn that word and why did she think Brandon was her daddy?

"No, baby, that's not daddy. That's Brandon, mommy's friend. Can you say *Bran-don*?" I ask trying to stop her dead in her tracks from giving him that title.

"No, mama," she insists, crossing her arms with a scowl on her face. "Dada."

She stares me down as if ready for battle but moments later her face brightens as Elmo starts to sing his theme song, *Elmo's World*, on the TV screen behind her. She walks back over to her Dora plush chair and plops herself down to give the show her full attention. I, on the other hand cannot not move. Thank goodness, no one else is around to witness what I imagine were my eyes popping out of my head. After a few minutes, I get my breath back and am able to clear my mind. Why would she call Brandon daddy? Who taught her that word? I mean, it is not as if I use it with her. And how did she know to make the connection of the title "daddy" to a male?

I make a mental note to ask Carm if she knows anything about this and I realize I have mixed emotions about it. How wonderful would it be if Brandon did become her daddy? My mind drifts off to a vision of Brandon, Angel and me at a park where we are taking turns pushing Angel on a swing while the other jumps into the air to touch her feet as she soars, laughing with glee, towards the clouds.

"Stop it, Aaron!" I command myself in a low tone so Angel cannot hear.

I definitely need to get my head on straight. Maybe it was not such a good idea to go and see Brandon after all. All of this crap is too much.

"Don't fight your destiny," I hear inside of me.

There it is again, that voice. At least I think I heard a voice because as quickly as it came, it is gone. What and who is that? Am I going crazy?

I pull out my BlackBerry and dial Carm's number. She answers after one ring.

"Hey Carm, it's me."

"What's up, Aaron? You better not be calling to cancel because I am almost ready," she says quickly, in a matter of fact tone. "I'm counting on this money because there is a BCBG dress I want so bad!"

"I'm not calling to cancel, Carm, relax. Actually, do you think you can come over earlier today? I need you to watch Angel while I get ready," I say.

"No problem. I can leave in ten if you want. How come you need me to be there while you get ready?" she asks. "That's not like you."

"Well, umm, I need to look extra special for a date tonight and I can't give Angel the attention she needs right now," I say, a little put off by her question.

"Enough said. I'm on my way. Bye," she says hanging up.

There. Done. That voice, as weird as this may seem, inspired me to get up and get out as quickly as possible. I need to get myself done up nice today and

I need time to get my courage drink in before I see Brandon. I think rum and Red Bull will do it for me.

Something in the core of my being is telling me that tonight is going to be a special night. I pick up Angel and carry her over to my closet so I can find something to wear. I open up the massive closet that stretches almost from wall to wall on one side of my room. Last year, I had a contractor come in and open up a wall that separated two closets and turn it into one humongous wardrobe. Then he installed a closet system. The result is a beautiful woman cave and a dream space.

I stand in front of the dress section. I am very proud of my collection of clothes and keep everything neatly organized by category and colour with two full rows of shoes lined up underneath. All of my jewellery is displayed in the centre-shelving unit that runs from the top to the bottom of the closet. It also separates my top wear from bottom wear for better display.

Ruby does not understand why all these details in my home are so important to me. But, growing up, these are all the things I wanted. If we did not always move and lived a normal life, I probably would have had them. My dad's criminal lifestyle had me used to being woken up in the middle of the night and leaving everything behind. If I was lucky, I would grab underwear and a toothbrush, but it had to be fast.

That is when I started packing my emergency bag, in which I kept three outfits, complete with underwear, socks, toothbrush and toothpaste. Settling down and having my own space to do as I pleased was one of my greatest accomplishments.

"Baby girl, mommy needs to look extra pretty tonight. You want to help mama find a dress?" I ask her in a voice that matches her baby tones.

"Pretty," she says as she reaches to pull on my black strapless dress with silver undertones.

I envision the dress on my body, remembering how well it fit and I am pleased.

"Good job, baby. This dress is perfect!" I say as I raise her little hand for a soft high five.

Wow, my little girl has fashion insight. This dress is exactly what I need for tonight. She pulled out my self-proclaimed freakum dress! I have only worn this piece twice and both times I blocked traffic—literally. It hugs me in the right places, accentuates the right curves and best of all, can be worn without a bra (my perky little girls standing at attention look extra hot in it when my nipples are hard). The length catches me mid-thigh and shows off my long, shapely legs. Paired with my silver stilettos and bam—freakum! This is exactly what the doctor ordered.

I put Angel on the floor and stand in front of my full-length mirror with the dress cradled against my body. Even if Brandon resents me, this dress would change that. I know I have crazy sex appeal and I own it. This dress would only add to making me a total package. A knock at my door snaps me out of my thoughts. Nice, Carm is here. It is time for my transformation. I head to the door, humming Beyoncé's song *Freakum Dress*.

Brandon is not going to know what hit him tonight!

Six † Brandon

Brandon checked his watch for what he imagined was the thousandth time as he leaned on the wall beside a table in the VIP section of the club. This was the normal spot where he met Aaron every Thursday and she was late.

He was afraid she was not going to show up but he hoped that she would. He had a plan to win her heart, but it would fail if she were a no-show because he might not have the courage to go through with it if he did not execute it tonight.

She was over an hour late and he was starting to accept that she was not coming. With a deep sigh of regret, he pulled out his wallet to pay for his drink and leave, but a familiar voice halted his steps.

"Going somewhere, Scar?" she asked in a tone oozing with seduction.

He turned to look at her and his words flummoxed in his throat. Her outfit was killer. She had on a banging black and silver dress that showed off her immaculately shaped body and a pair of stilettos that could drive a clean hole through any surface. She wore her hair piled high on top of her head with a few mischievous curls that refused to be tamed hanging loosely. He loved how her hairstyle showed off her beautiful neck and spotlighted the tiny birthmark that looked like a dot on her collarbone. Her eyes were piercing into his as if she had a story to tell.

"Ahhh, look who decided to honour me with her presence," he said jokingly as he pulled her in for a warm hug.

She felt so right and fit perfectly against him. He wished he could hold her there forever.

"I'm glad you came!" he said not bothering to try to contain how pleased he was to see her.

"What's wrong, baby? I thought men expected women to be late for a date?" she asked him playfully as she threw her arms around his neck again and pulled him in for another tight squeeze.

Something was off about her today, Brandon thought. She was being too nice and too, well, cuddly. He welcomed the change but was a bit worried about the true intentions of her affection. Was she setting him up for revenge for the cruel things he said to her during their last encounter?

Whatever it was, he was not going to let her throw off his plan. He had to stay firm and strong for everything to work out the way he wanted. It almost felt like life or death to him because he loved her and had to earn her love. Yes, he loved her. He realized it for the first time yesterday as he sat devising his plan to win her over. Thinking so deeply about her, he was overcome by sentiment he never knew existed. He never even felt this way about his ex-wife. Without having to be told, he knew it was love.

"I am glad you came, Aaron. That's all that matters," he said in a serious tone as he pulled away from their embrace to face her and meet her eyes. "I'm sorry about the other day, really sorry."

"Let's not talk about that, Scar," she said a little too quickly. "I'm ready to bump and grind!"

Right on cue, one of his favourite old school songs came pouring out of the speakers with a beat that allowed his body to move easily. *It Takes Two* was his jam since he was a kid. He led her onto the floor to dance with him. As they moved effortlessly to the song, he loved how she made faces and mouthed the words as if she was Rob Base. Her body flowed with the beat as if it was specifically produced for her rhythm and timing. He grooved and moved on the dance floor until he was behind her and pulled her body into his so they could move as one. When the song was over, he led her back over to his table in the VIP section. Normally, they would have drinks and dance the night away. Then they would retire with the sunrise for an intimate encounter. Tonight was going to be different. It was all part of the plan. He grabbed his jacket and pulled it on.

"Are...we...going somewhere?" she asked, obviously puzzled by the change of routine.

"I want to do something different tonight. Put your jacket on and let's go." he said placing his hand softly on her lower back, urging her to play along.

They walked out into the cool night. Although it was mid-July, the nights were cooler than the days when the sun ravished them with the gift of heat. Luckily, the club was close to one of his favourite restaurants that would serve well to create the atmosphere Brandon needed to set off his plan. A few minutes later, they arrived at the darkly lit and intimate Caribbean restaurant, and he opened the door for her to enter. The round tables and dark velvet covered chairs added a nice hit of elegance to the establishment. Each table had a beautiful Swarovski crystal chandelier hanging above it but there were no light bulb fixtures. Instead, candle centerpieces on each table gave off just enough light to create the perfect playhouse for romance. He gave his name to the gracious host and they were led to a table in a nice corner of the restaurant. He took her jacket and pulled out her chair.

"What's all this?" she asked in a low voice trying not to attract the attention of the couples around them. "Why are we here?"

"I thought we could do something different tonight. I'm getting tired of the same old club scene and I haven't eaten any dinner yet," Brandon said.

"Well, I wish I knew your plans ahead of time because I would have dressed...differently," she replied in a voice that gave away her insecurities.

He noticed her eyes scanning the room to look at the other women in the restaurant who were dressed more conservatively than her. He did not care and thought she was the best-dressed woman.

"Baby, don't worry, you look beautiful." He smiled at her and squeezed her hand for reassurance, "None of these women can compare to you!"

She appeared to relax instantly at his encouragement. Just then, a waiter approached their table with two tri-folded menus.

"Good evening. I am Paul and I will be your server for the night. Tonight's special is lobster tails in black bean sauce served with jasmine rice," he said with a slight West Indian accent. "I also recommend the curried shrimp with mango sauce, which is a very popular dish. Can I get you something to drink while you look over the menu?"

"Yes, please," said Brandon. "A Cosmo for the beautiful lady and a rum and Coke for myself. We'll need about five minutes to look over the menus."

"Very good," he said. "I'll be right back with your drinks." He walked off towards the bar.

Aaron looked at the menu as though it was a burden to her eyes.

"Everything looks so yummy; I have no idea what to order."

"Well, I normally order the curry shrimp and mango sauce but I know you love your chicken breast. They make a tasty chicken breast and pineapple dish with their notorious rum sauce. Trust me, sweetie, it's to die for," Brandon told her.

"Well, that's what I'll have," she said with a slight smile.

Brandon smiled back but she quickly lowered her eyes. Her personality seemed to shrink within this atmosphere. As she stared past him, avoiding eye contact, Brandon wondered what she was thinking about. She appeared to be in a trance-like state.

"What's on your mind?" he asked her gently.

She looked up at him and then shook her head.

"Nothing, I guess. Well, I mean, I guess I was in a party mood and not a dinner mood. I'll be fine though, don't worry about me," she said.

"Good!" Brandon answered, relieved that she was willing to stay.

The dinner went well. The meals were delicious and they both enjoyed three drinks each. He never knew she had such a great sense of humour and they giggled and laughed the night away. A few times, there was a tiny bit of awkwardness as his leg grazed hers or her hand brushed his. He could feel the sexual tension building between them, especially since the alcohol took the edge off everything. They both enjoyed a pastry dessert topped with rum and raisin ice cream and then Brandon made eye contact with the waiter to signal that he was ready for the bill.

"I parked just a little way up this street," he said as they left the restaurant.

They walked hand in hand for a bit then he pulled her in closer so he could wrap his strong arm around her shoulders. She smiled at the warmth of his embrace and nuzzled her head under his chin.

They got into the car and she immediately reached over to rub his spot, as she normally did to get him aroused on the car ride home. This time, he intercepted her hand and pulled it up to his lips for a kiss. She looked startled.

"Something wrong, Scar?" she asked with a slight pout on her lips.

He could tell by her reaction that she felt rejected.

"No, everything is fine," he answered with a charming smile as he continued to clasp her warm hand in his.

"O...kay," she said and slumped back into her seat, looking out the window.

He could feel her brain working overtime, trying to figure out why he rejected their familiar routine of passionate strokes that led to a fun and energetic night of coupling. As much as he longed for the familiar touch and probing, it did not fit into his ultimate plan.

It took him about twenty minutes to reach her apartment. Instead of turning a sharp right and driving into her parking spot behind the store as he normally did, he drove straight to the front entrance.

"Huh?" She didn't bother to hide her surprise, "You're not coming upstairs?"

"Not tonight, baby," he said as he leaned closer to her and brushed her cheek with his lips.

"Scar, what the heck is going on?" she said, her voice rising. "If you think you're not going to give me my money because you bought me dinner, you have another thing..."

She did not get to finish her sentence as he pulled a sealed envelope out of his inner pocket and handed it to her. He got out of the car, walked around and opened the door for her, reaching out his hand to help her out of the car. Then he walked the few steps with her to the front door.

"Goodnight, sweetie," he said as he pulled her in for a long embrace.

When he finally let her go, she looked confused and frustrated.

"Scar, what's wrong? Are you still upset about the other night? Is this your way of getting back at me?" she said angrily and then added in a whisper, "Did I do something wrong?"

"No, Aaron, nothing is wrong. Everything is perfect. Have a good night, beautiful. See you soon," he said, pecking her briefly on her cheek before leaving.

It took Brandon everything he had not to turn around and go back after he glanced in the rear-view mirror and saw her staring after him like a lost puppy. She looked so sad and that was not a part of his plan. He wanted to comfort her and pleasure her beyond her wildest imagination but he could not. He took one last look in the mirror, and then accelerated and flew out of sight. He had to, before he reconsidered.

His love for her overpowered his longing for her body and he knew to win her heart and become her Prince Charming; he had to treat her like a regular woman. It was due time she understood her worth.

Yeah, he still paid the same amount he would have paid for their regular 'dates' but it was all part of his plan. He knew she was a business minded and still had to feel secure with her finances.

Until he won her heart, he promised himself he would have no more sexual encounters with her. It was the right thing to do. Well, he prayed it was the right thing. It was risky plan but he had to take a chance.

Seven † Aaron

I sit silently in the dark going over the events of the night in my head. What did I do wrong? What did I do to turn him off? I am so confused.

The night started perfectly. I left early so I could stop at my favourite salon for a top to bottom beauty treatment. I had my hair, nails and toes done and then stopped at a bar close by to have a few courage drinks.

I wanted to take our relationship to a different level of intimacy and I thought this was the only way to do it. Yes, I was late for our date but that did not seem like a good reason to blow me off. Let me think: dancing in the club, a beautiful and fun dinner during which I felt we connected and then...nothing. He dropped me off at the front door and practically burned rubber to get out of there. Gosh, did I smell? I lift my arms for a pit check. I know my hygiene is not the problem but I was secretly hoping for something obvious to put me out of the misery of not knowing.

I was actually looking forward to a night of intimacy with him that would be unlike previous nights when I just did—my job. Even now, the thought of him pressed against me gives me delightful shots of sensuality up and down my body. I cannot believe this. I have never felt this way before. What is happening?

I force myself to get up off the couch to take a shower. I need a cold one to calm my hot body and racing heart. After five minutes under the water, the shower only manages to cool my sexual drive but does nothing for my wounded heart and ego.

Wrapped in a towel, I walk over to my purse to retrieve my cell phone to call him and find out the underlying cause of everything. But the envelope he handed me in the car catches my eye. Oh, it makes sense now. He probably shortchanged me. I tear it open and my money is there—all of it. It is the card in the envelope, however, that I am focusing on. On the front of the card is an image of a beautiful Nubian Queen, garnished with gold. I quickly open the card to find the words: "You are worth more than all the gold in the world. Stay beautiful. Brandon."

I feel the hot sting of tears trying to escape from my eyes. I quickly blink them away as I read and reread what he wrote. Brandon thought I was worth more than gold. Was this some kind of joke? As I sit meditating on what he wrote, I allow my mind to drift back to my life before that dreadful day.

"Push me higher, daddy, higher!" I squealed in delight as my father pushed me on the new swing set he bought for me. "I want to touch the sky."

"All right, princess," he said. "Hang on tight because this push is going to get you there."

"Wheeeeeeeee!" I exclaimed in delight as he pushed me and ran underneath the swing to help me reach the height I wanted. "Yay, daddy! You are the best!"

We played all afternoon. I was around six-years-old. My daddy loved me more than anything. I knew this because he always said he loved me more than gold and my daddy loved his gold. He had three gold teeth, gold rings all over his fingers and gold accented many areas in our home. I had to be something special for someone to love me more than that. At least I thought I was special before that night....

"You are special," says that voice in my mind, jolting me from my thoughts. "You have and will always be special to me. He sees you how I designed you to be."

I am completely shaken out of my memories by a gripping fear. Not now, not the crazy voice again. I cannot handle it tonight. And who is the *He* the voice is referring to? Is it Brandon? What did it mean by the way it designed me? I was not designed by anybody. Not only am I crazy, but the voice is crazy too!

A tear slowly falls from my eyes as I hold onto those last moments of my memories. I quickly wipe it away, refusing to give into any more foolish emotions tonight.

I look at the card again and think that Brandon should not throw statements and words around so carelessly just for sex. But if sex was his goal then he would have come upstairs with me tonight. Could Brandon actually feel this way about me for real? Better yet, why would he feel this way about a whore?

Maybe, just maybe, if that night did not happen when I was younger, I would be worthy of that kind of affection. I would have grown up respected and loved. I would have finished school and became a designer like I wanted to, and my life would have counted. All that was taken away from me on that horrific night. Why did it have to happen? Why did anyone not care? It hurt so badly.

"What is that?" I ask myself as my purse starts to buzz noisily.

Oh, my cell phone is receiving a text. It better not be Ruby; I am not in the mood for her right now. The message is from Brandon:

HOPE U HAD A GOOD TIME TNIGHT. I DID ☺
SLEEP TIGHT & DREAM OF ME. B

I pull my phone into my chest and hug it. He had a good time tonight. I did not do anything wrong.   Instantly, my insecurities vanish. He had to be thinking of me to send me a text. He never sent me this kind of text before.

I have a warm, fuzzy feeling inside that I cannot quench, and it is not sexual. I am really feeling him. Maybe, I could change my life and become that woman I know I was meant to be. Maybe Brandon can love me. Maybe he does not look at me with the same eyes as every other male in the world. Maybe he can look past my exterior and like the person I am inside.

I lay back on my couch and snuggle deeply into my plush robe. I start to fantasize about me and Brandon lying on the couch, holding each other while Angel plays on the rug in front of us. I fall asleep, allowing my dreams to become my reality for the night.

Eight † Ruby

Ring, ring, ring.

"Damn it, Aaron," Ruby muttered to herself. "Answer the phone."

"Hmmm, hello?" Aaron answered, her voice groggy with sleep.

"Yo, where the hell have you been? I've been calling you and calling you and you haven't answered the phone!" Ruby replied without bothering to cover up how pissed off she was.

"Oh, I've been pretty busy. You know, making them papers," Aaron said with a hint of annoyance in her voice.

"So, what, you can't answer your phone?" demanded Ruby.

"Girl please, relax. I was busy. Enough said. I answered now, right?"

Ruby could not believe the way Aaron was talking to her. She was certainly not used to this since Aaron usually sucked up to her.

"Who do you think you're talking to, Aaron? Don't you ever forget who I am! Plus, I know you weren't out there making any papers because I saw one of your customers on the street and he told me you stood him up last night!"

"Um, so what, Ruby, are you calling me a liar?" asked Aaron. "Since when do I have to report everything I do to you? I'm a grown woman!"

"Really? All of a sudden, you're grown huh? Remember, Aaron, I made you and I can destroy you!" screamed Ruby.

"You know what? I'm tired and not in the mood for a cat fight so call me when you're in a better mood!" shouted Aaron and then the line went dead.

Ruby sat frozen with the phone still at her ear. Did Aaron just hang up the phone on her? She quickly redialed the number and after four rings got Aaron's familiar voice mail message: *Sorry I missed your call but that's life. Leave a message after the beep.*

"Damn it," Ruby said aloud. "Since when is she ignoring my calls? What happened? It's like an overnight change."

Ruby walked over to the fridge, took out a pint of Rocky Road ice cream, grabbed a spoon and headed into her bedroom to wallow in pity on her queen size bed. She could not believe how Aaron spoke to her but worse than that, she felt as if Aaron was slipping away. Ever since the day that Scar dude and her got into their little argument, Ruby had noticed differences in Aaron, like talking about changing her life and everything. As she brought a huge spoonful of ice cream into her mouth, Ruby longed for Aaron to be with her, a spoon of her own in hand, watching their favourite television shows on TV. Aaron was her only female friend and truth be told; she was more than a friend. Ruby loved her as though she were her little sister.

Ever since that wonderful night she met Aaron in the alley rummaging through the garbage, her life changed and all of a sudden, it had meaning. She became Aaron's protector, big sister and best friend. Before that, she had only existed day-to-day, waiting for someone who had it even harder than she did to take her out on the streets. Ruby was actually willing that day to come. This sick, dirty, pathetic life was not for her, but it was all she had. Aaron had changed all that by making her feel like a big sister again. She still longed for the touch and smell of her own beautiful baby sister...

"Ruby! Where are you with that damn bottle?" her mom shouted from the living room. Her baby sister was only two months old then and Ruby had always wanted a sibling.

"Coming, ma!" Ruby shouted from the kitchen.

Her mom did not believe in breastfeeding, or so she said. Even at the age of 10, Ruby knew that her mom's breast milk would not be a healthy choice for her precious little sister—her sister with no name. Ruby's mom was annoyed by the baby and could not stand to have her around. She had left the hospital without naming the baby. Two months later, she still claimed she could not think of a suitable name. Mom was a crack head and conceived her sister with one of her suppliers. She did not know which one. She even tried and tried to do things to lose the baby during her pregnancy, but it did not work. Ruby had prayed and prayed during the pregnancy that God would protect the baby so she could have a family. Her grandmother used to teach her about God before she died and took her to church with her a few times. Her grandmother was the only blood relative she had because mama had been an only child and grandpa died before Ruby was born.

Mama was always gone and when she was home, Ruby stayed as far away from her as possible. Today, mama was in the room with another one of those *uncles*. As Ruby went into the room to bring mama the bottle, she noticed the man in the room was weird looking with his frizzy hair, long mustache and gap in his teeth. Chills ran up and down Ruby's spine every time he smiled at her.

"Mama, do you want me to take the baby into my room with me?" Ruby asked quietly, hoping her mama would say yes.

It was past her bedtime but she loved and cherished any moment she could have with her sister.

"Nah...you go to bed. I'm gonna need you to get up in the night when the baby gets up so go get your rest now," her mom said.

"Okay, mama," Ruby said as she turned to leave the room. "If you need me, call me."

When she got to the door, she turned around and ran back to give her baby sister a warm kiss.

"Love you, baby."

Her baby sister smiled at her with what seemed like so much love in her eyes. She was so adorable and although she wanted to stay, Ruby ran out of the room before her mom could yell at her.

The next morning, Ruby jumped up with a start. Something was wrong. The sun was out and the baby had not woken up to cry for milk. Every night since the baby had come home, Ruby got up to make her a bottle. Why had the baby not woken up and cried last night? Ruby got out of bed to go check on the baby. The weird guy was gone and her mom was passed out on the bed. She tiptoed over to check on her baby sister and witnessed the most horrific sight. Paralyzed by shock, she started screaming uncontrollably until she passed out. When she finally came to, police officers were all around and she was taken from her home and placed in a group home for girls. Two years passed before one of the workers finally took pity on her and told her what happened to her sister.

Ruby's mom had put the baby in the crib with the bottle propped up on a pillow to feed her so she could do her lines of coke. She was knocked out cold from the drugs and forgot to burp the baby, who suffocated on her own vomit. By the time Ruby went to check on her in the morning, the blue and swollen baby had been dead for a few hours.

When her mother called 9-1-1 after Ruby went into shock, the police found drugs all over the apartment, including in her mother's bed.

Ruby only saw her mom once after that, when the caseworkers brought her to visit her in jail. Four years later, her mother still blamed Ruby and her baby sister for her jail sentence. They had ruined her life. She never wanted kids—especially not girls.

At the tender age of fourteen, Ruby turned and walked out of the jail and her mother's life that day. She never looked back and managed to slip the childcare worker and run away. She had been on the streets ever since.

The bitterness she felt towards her mom and God resurfaced. If God existed, why did he take her baby sister away? She was the only hope for Ruby to have someone to love.

Now, she was losing Aaron, the only other person in her life she cared about.

Ruby dropped her head in her hands and did something she had not done since her sister died, she wept until she was empty.   She felt so alone. Ruby finally wiped her nose on her sleeve and wiped away any sign of tears with the back of her hand. She could only imagine how pathetic and weak she must look right now.

"Hell no!" she yelled at her reflection when she finally pulled herself up off the bed to survey her appearance in the mirror.

She made a promise to herself that she was going to find out what was going on with Aaron and get rid of the problem. She lost one sister already. She refused to lose another. She did not care who got hurt in the process. She only knew that this time, it would not be her.

Nine † Aaron

"**D**ang, leave me alone," I shout at my phone as I press the ignore button.

It is my Tuesday night customer calling—again. I have not seen him in over three weeks. Actually, I have not seen anyone besides Brandon in the last three weeks even on the days I normally reserved for my other customers. It just felt like the right thing to do. Since that wonderful night we shared, I have not been able to bring myself to service any other men. The thought grosses me out. Brandon makes me feel like I am better than that. When I am with him now, I do not feel like a prostitute. Over the last three weeks, he wined and dined me, took me on picnics, to an amusement park, and so much more. He has not petitioned me for sex and he still pays me. There is no more leaving money on the table; he now presents it like a gift. At the end of each date, Brandon gives me an envelope with a card that always has a special design on the outside and a personal message from him inside. A few times, the envelope was coupled with flowers or a box of expensive chocolates.

I cannot remember laughing so much in my life—real, hearty laughter. The other day I laughed so hard the pop I was drinking flew out my nose. It only made us laugh even harder.

I have a date with Brandon tonight and it is going to be special because I have made a firm decision that I want to share with him. I cannot believe how much stronger my feelings for him have become in only three weeks but it has been three weeks of pure bliss. I am going to tell Brandon I want to take our relationship to another level. I do not want him to pay me anymore. I want to be with him, no strings attached. I want to be his girlfriend.

The very thought of being in a relationship with him makes me giggle like a schoolgirl and the thought of changing my life makes me feel that there is hope for me after all. I am not sure how I am going to make money but I will figure something out. I have a healthy savings account that can carry me for a while and I am going to find a job—a real job.

I have never had a legitimate job in my life but there has to be something I can do. The more I think about my decision, the better I feel.

I am not just doing this for me, it is for Angel too because I want her to grow up in a normal environment and be proud of me. She will never have to know about the things I did, I will never tell her. It will be for her own good. I need to protect my baby.

I get a new text message alert and smile when I look at the screen and see that it is from Brandon:

DON'T DRESS UP 2NIGHT. CASUAL. BRING ANGEL. B

Huh? What the? Bring Angel? What did Brandon have up his sleeve for tonight?

Oh, you may have noticed, I have decided not to refer to him as Scar anymore.   Brandon is such a beautiful name and it suits him. I have not even seen his scar in a long time and I miss it. I long for intimacy with him. I crave his touch. I yearn for him to hold me passionately again. For some reason, no matter how hard I try, he will not go there with me. Sometimes I do not know what to do because I am an expert in sex but inexperienced in romance. Brandon is taking the lead and although I am not used to it yet, I like the feeling. I am crossing my fingers that my proclamation will make him want me tonight, but bringing Angel is not part of my plan. I reply to his text:

HEY B. WHAT R UR PLANS 4 TONIGHT? A

U DON'T NEED 2 KNOW, LOL. U R 2 NOSEY. B

I smile. I love this playful side of him. He always makes me feel so comfortable. It looks like I have no other option but to include Angel into my plan.

I head over to the crib to check on Angel who is fast asleep. I know the perfect outfit for her to wear today. I bought her the cutest little cotton candy pink dress with spaghetti straps and ruffles. Her curly hair is finally at a length that allows me to style it in two neat ponytails. She will look so adorable that Brandon will not be able to turn down my proposal.

I look around my place and instantly feel a wonderful sensation about the way it looks. I wonder again if it is possible for me to find a job doing some kind of decorating. It is the only thing I can think of that I really love and I am naturally good at it.

My phone starts ringing again. I wonder if it is Brandon or Carm. That reminds me, I need to let Carm know I do not need her to baby-sit tonight.

"Hello?" I answer anxiously, without checking the caller display.

"What's popping?" Ruby replies.

Dang! I pause for a moment to catch myself and compose my thoughts. I have been avoiding Ruby for that last couple of weeks because I do not know how to tell her about my decision.

"Not much. How are you?" I ask under the false pretense that I really care.

Sure, I know I am being selfish right now but I have a hard time picturing Ruby in my mental blueprint of a new life. She would have to change her life as well or she would serve as a daily reminder of what I am trying to walk away from.

"I'm alright. I'm surprised you care though. You've been avoiding me like the plague," she sighs deeply, causing me to feel a twinge of guilt. "Did I do something wrong?"

"No, girl, it's not you. It is definitely me!"

I realize how cheesy that sounds. I take a deep breath to build up the guts to say what I really need to say. Then, in fear of losing my courage, I blurt it all out at once:

"The truth is...I don't want to work the streets no more. I want to change my life and be square. I need to do this for Angel and for my sanity. I am going to find myself a real job, something Angel can be proud of when she's old enough to understand."

Whew! I did it. There is a moment of awkward silence that has me a little worried but Ruby finally speaks up.

"So, just to get this straight in my head, you want to stop working the streets and you plan on getting a real job?"

"That's right," I say, a little too low.

"And you are saying that you want...to...be...*square*?" she asks.

"Yup, that's right," I say, with a little more confidence.

There is another brief moment of silence. Butterflies are multiplying in my stomach now but I refuse to give in to my fear. I glance in Angel's direction to remind myself why I need to stay strong.

"Is this the reason why you have been avoiding me?" Ruby asks.

"Well, yeah," I answer, a little thrown off by this unexpected question. "I didn't know how to tell you this. I figured you would be pissed off. "

This time it was Ruby's turn to take a deep breath which she let out slowly.

"Aaron, I'm not pissed off at you for you wanting to change your life. I'm happy about that. I'm pissed off that you don't trust me enough to know that I always have your back, no matter what." Ruby sounds genuinely hurt.

I think her words over for a minute before admitting to myself that she is right. After knowing her for so many years and trusting her with so much, I did not even give her the benefit of the doubt. I decide there is no time like the present to put her to the ultimate test.

"Ruby, you know your most important rule about not dating squares, especially not customers? Well, I tore that rule to shreds." I say with a shaky voice because the butterflies have now taken over my insides. "I am kind of...well...dating Brandon."

"Brandon? Who's Brandon?" she asks. But before I can answer, she says, "You mean— Scar?"

"Yes. That's Brandon," I answer defensively.

There is an awkward silence. My tummy feels the same way it did when Brandon took me on the Drop Zone ride at Canada's Wonderland amusement park and I was anticipating the plunge. Then she says something for which I am not prepared:

"Aaron, that's amazing! I am so happy for you!"

I feel a ton of pent up emotions release from my body as all the butterflies dissipate. I cannot believe I ever doubted Ruby, even for a moment. Tears spring to my eyes. With that, I tell Ruby everything that happened over the last three weeks, sparing her no details. After about an hour of conversation, Ruby hangs up the phone, promising to set up a girls' spa night so we can celebrate my great news.

I do not think I ever felt as much love for Ruby as I do right now. Today, I truly understand how much she loves and cares for me. She is supporting me even though I broke her number one rule. Forget one rule, I broke them all!

I wrap myself in my own arms and rock from side to side with glee. It looks like I can have Brandon in my life and Ruby too. Life cannot get any better than this.

Ten † Ruby

Ruby threw the phone across the room with so much force that she would not have been surprised if it smashed to a thousand pieces. Right now, she could not care less.

She knew something was up with Aaron but nothing could have prepared her for what she was told.

"That ungrateful little bitch!" Ruby screamed as she paced back and forth in her home.

After everything Ruby did for her, she let a custy take her away so easily. Well, Aaron had another thing coming if she thought Ruby was going to sit back and let it happen—no way! Ruby blamed herself. She should have caught on and did something about it when she first noticed Aaron's mood change that day in the Eaton Centre. Then, she had the nerve to be fantasizing about her Prince Charming. Prince Charming my ass, she thought. How could Scar be her Prince Charming? What a joke. Aaron's highest paying customer is now the man of her dreams? Give me a break! On top of all that, now she did not want him to pay her anymore.

Ruby had to hand it to Scar. He was a smart one. After paying for Aaron's services for a year he figured out how to get into her pants for free. Ruby cringed thinking about how Aaron corrected her when she called Brandon, Scar. Ruby needed to high five Scar when she saw him and hand him an award for being the cleverest man on earth.

"Over my dead body," Ruby screamed once again as she stopped to examine a picture she had of Aaron and Angel on her side table. "How can you be so damn naïve?"

She knew what people like Scar were about. He would use Aaron and after she was hooked, he would ditch her and Ruby would be left to pick up the pieces. How clever of him to know that refusing sex from Aaron for three weeks would make her feel special. There was no way Ruby going to let that happen to Aaron. She would do everything she could to protect her.

Ruby had already started shaping a strategy to fix the problem while she was listening to Aaron ramble on about Scar for over an hour. Listening to all that sappiness made her want to cut her own throat.

Her plan was simple. First, Ruby had to remind Aaron of her skills. Having intercourse with men was her best talent. It was obvious to Ruby that lack of sex had Aaron thinking she was square. Ruby would set her up for a night she would not forget under the false pretense of a celebration spa date. She knew what she had to do and she knew the two people who would be more than willing to help execute her plan. Oh, Aaron would get her celebration party, all right! After that, she would never, ever forget who she is and for what she was made.

Ruby got up to retrieve the cell phone she had hurled moments earlier thankful it was still intact. She pulled up her contact list, found and dialed the number she needed, and heard a gruff voice answer after three rings.

"Who dis?"

"What's up, G? It's Ruby. How you been?"

"Ruby? Yo, I'm good, especially now that I hear your lovely voice," he answered.

Ruby smiled. This is going to be way too easy.

"Baby", she said, "you know my girl Aaron? She is feeling you—really feeling you. She wants to celebrate a milestone in her life and I gave her my word that I could get you to celebrate by having an all-nighter with her at a fancy hotel. There is one catch though. She wants you to bring a friend. The girl is a freak..."

"Oh yeah?" he said before she could finish her sentence, "Baby, you don't need to ask me twice. I know the perfect person for that. Damn, a threesome. It's been awhile since I had me one of those."

"Calm down G, lemme finish. About that freak thing, she wants to do a role-play type of game. You know, to fulfill her fantasy. She is going to pretend as if she doesn't want the ish to go down. You're gonna have to get rough with her but don't worry, it's all good," Ruby said and held her breath.

"Whoa!" G said. "I don't know about all of that. I don't force myself on anyone. Nobody wanna go to jail or nothing.'"

"This is what I mean, baby, by doing me a favour. She wants to live out this fantasy. You have nothing to worry about, G. You know as well as I know that you can't rape a whore, right?" Ruby said with a devilish grin. "You have to trust me on this one."

He seemed to think it over briefly before he agreed.

"That's right, baby, for a minute I forgot she's a streetwalker. One of the best I heard. She is different from the other girls though. She carries herself differently...you know...like a lady." Then he added, "Hey, you don't expect me to pay for this, do you?"

"Nah," she said. "You know that money you owe me for getting you the bag of weed? Consider it settled."

"That's all right with me," he said. "I just need to know when and where."

"I'll call you later and let you know exactly what's up. Bye, G," she ended the call.

For a moment, Ruby felt guilty about her plan. What was she thinking? What was she doing? A flash of her baby sister, blue and swollen, in the crib appeared in her mind. No, she had to do this, she convinced herself. She had to save Aaron. This was the only way.

She picked up the phone again to book a room in a ritzy downtown hotel she often frequented. Her inside contact, Dennis, always gave her luxury suites at a fraction of the cost if she paid him cash.

"Hey, Dennis, my man. It's Ruby. I need a huge favour. Give me some dates that my favourite honeymoon suite is available for a full weekend. I'm gonna need it again for a special client."

Ruby listened to his response and then replied, "No problem, I am willing to give you a double payment for your trouble, as usual. You know the deal."

She thanked him and hung up the phone thinking about how much money she was losing to set up this night. As if losing the one thousand dollars G owed her for the bag of weed she scored for him was not enough, now she had to pay Dennis double. That would be seventeen hundred dollars in total. Well, she knew it was worth it. She would pay a million dollars to save her friend from herself. Yes, she told herself, this was for Aaron's good. After all, she loved Aaron with her entire heart.

Eleven † Brandon

Brandon was excited to see Aaron today and even more excited about Angel.   There was something so captivating about her. She was a sweet little girl and so full of joy. Aaron was blessed to have her.

Brandon had wanted a child of his own but Tanika had not been so keen on the idea. She boldly stated one romantic night in the midst of toasting their perfect life with a bottle of Gran Patron Platinum Silver Tequila that she liked their family at the size it was. This threw Brandon off because when they met, they discussed life with children and she showed enthusiasm equally matched to his. Sharing passions for the same things in relationships was important to Brandon and one of the reasons he married Tanika. It seemed like many of her interests changed after he *put a ring on it*. It was a continuous joke amongst some of his friends about how gullible he really was.

He had a special day planned for Aaron, which he naturally felt should include Angel. Since his divorce, he had not brought any other woman into his home. He was grateful when Tanika let him buy her out during the divorce settlement. He felt the time was right to welcome Aaron into his private space. Anytime they got together in the past, they either went to a hotel or back to her charming, well-decorated apartment.

Brandon walked over to the stove to see how his pasta sauce was coming along. He was preparing a five-course meal that he planned to serve and feed her. He wanted her to feel like a queen today.

For the millionth time in the last three weeks, Brandon gushed warmly over how well things were progressing between them. It felt like an overnight change. Granted, it was all part of his strategy to win her heart but it almost seemed too easy. Sometimes, an insecure voice in his head told him she was setting him up for failure and that playing along was her tactic to get back at him for the unforgivable things he said to her during their argument. His heart on the other hand told him this was no game and they were so compatible because they were made for each other. It felt like she was designed just for him. Everything about her excited him and he could not find any flaws in her personality or her appearance.

Brandon picked up the phone in the kitchen and dialed his mother's cell phone number for the fourth time in the last hour.

"Hi Mom, me again."

His mom suppressed a giggle. "Hello again, dear son of mine. So which one is it? Did you burn the sauce or the pasta noodles?"

"Ha, ha, Mom, very funny." Brandon responded in a voice that matched her playful tone. "I have another quick question for you. The sauce is finished so do I turn down the stove or turn it off completely?"

"If she'll be there soon, you can leave it on simmer. If it will be awhile, you can turn it off and warm it up again."

"Okay, Mom. Thanks again, my lovely."

Brandon blew his mom a kiss before hanging up the phone. He realized that just because a man wanted to cook a meal to wine and dine the woman who owns his heart did not necessarily make him an expert chef. At least with his mom's helpful advice and coaching, he was able to prepare a decent meal. He was proud of himself.

Brandon was satisfied as he looked around at everything he prepared. All he had left to do was clean up the mess he made on the granite countertops and load the dishwasher. When he was finished, he called Aaron, eager to leave and pick her up. She answered right away and he heard Angel in the background making a huge fuss.

"Hey baby, what's wrong with the little princess?"

"She's upset because I'm combing her hair. I'm trying to put it into a ponytail," Aaron said.

Brandon thought about Angel's wild and flowing head of hair, adorned with the springiest curls he ever saw in his life. The thought of it being styled seemed wrong. He loved her gorgeous head of hair.

"Leave her hair alone. Didn't I tell you it was a casual event? That means Angel too. I am looking forward to seeing her big puff of hair!" he said with a snicker.

"Okay, Brandon. You win," she said and Angel instantly stopped fussing.

The thought of Aaron releasing her from her grip and Angel hightailing it out of there made him chuckle.

"I just wanted to let you know that I'm leaving now and will be at your place in approximately half an hour. I'll call you when I'm close and you can meet me outside, unless you need help bringing anything down," he said.

"No, I'm good. See you soon."

"Bye."

Brandon headed to the front door but contemplated taking a quick swig of something to help calm his nerves. He decided against the idea— no drinking and driving for him. He did not know why but he was so nervous about today. She was an urban girl and he hoped she would accept his suburban lifestyle. If she did not, he was willing to change his style for her. She was that important to him.

Forty minutes later, Brandon pulled up outside her apartment. He jumped out the car, kissed both Aaron and Angel on the cheek and relieved Aaron of the car seat. He installed it in his car and strapped in Angel, who studied him intensely.

"Dada," she said as he finished clicking the seat belt in around her chubby little figure.

He almost swallowed his Dentyne peppermint flavored gum. He smiled and managed to respond with a tiny,"hi", which he accompanied by a twinkling motion with his fingers. It took everything in him not to rip her out of the car seat and dance around the driveway to a happy, soundless rhythm.

"Sorry about that," Aaron replied sheepishly, seeming both embarrassed and afraid that he would think she trained Angel to say that.

"Not a problem," he said not hiding his smile and leaned over and kissed her firmly on the lips.

He wanted her to know that he was more than OK with what just happened. In fact, he hoped Angel said it again.

Yup, he thought to himself, tonight is absolutely going to be a night to remember.

Twelve † Aaron

I can barely hold up the weight of my jaw as Brandon pulls up on his semi-circular cobblestone driveway, accented with a well-manicured front lawn. The trees in his front yard seemed to lift their arms to me as the birds in the sky serenaded me with sweet song.

The beauty of the outdoor landscape mesmerized me. Only in my dreams did a house like this actually exist. It was breathtaking. I get out of the car slowly as Brandon retrieves Angel from the back. There is nothing that can make me rush this moment. I feel so overwhelmed that my breath quickens as I deeply inhale a hit of fresh air. I lean against the side of the car and clasp my hands together.

"Welcome to my home," Brandon's proud voice snaps me out of my thoughts.

He must have noticed something is off about me because he looks at me worriedly and asks if I am okay. I can only nod my head in response. He props Angel up with one arm while she rests on his hip and slings the other arm around my tiny waist as he guides me up the front steps. I remain quiet.

If I thought the outside was dazzling, nothing could have prepared me for what I see as Brandon swings open the left side of the double door entry and guides me in with a gentle push on my lower back. I gasp aloud. My feet turn to liquid cement and then harden as they root firmly into the ground. I refuse to take another step forward because I simply cannot.

"You hate it, don't you?" says Brandon with a disappointed voice that again snaps me back to reality.

For a moment, I had totally forgotten where I was and whom I was with. My eyes glaze over and the concrete disappears from around my ankles, granting me mobility again.

"Hate it? No way, Brandon, it's perfect!" I say, walking over to him and throwing my arms around his neck.

Angel is already off exploring on her own and clearly does not care about what we are doing. She is much more forward than I am and has made her way over to a soft, brown leather bench, which she is trying to climb.

"Brandon, words can't explain how beautiful your home is. I'm speechless!" I shout, a little louder than intended.

Brandon smiles the most charming boyish smile I have ever seen. He wraps his arms around my waist and twirls me around.

"You don't understand how truly relieved I am to hear you say that!" he says, planting wet kisses all over my face.

How can the house from my dreams be real? I cannot begin to fathom this as I toy with the idea in my head. This is way too freaky.

Let me break down this house for you as Brandon gives me a tour. As soon as you step into the dark brown, heavy, antique double doorway, grey marble floors that take you from the front to the back of the house, greet you.   There is a grand staircase in the center of the home that branches off into two staircases that lead to the upper hallway.

The kitchen is in the back of the house and can you say marvelous? The rich brown colour of the cabinets matches the front doors and is accented with pewter-coloured handles in the shape of teardrops. The French doors in the back of the kitchen lead to a patio that is definitely styled for outdoor comfort. I have never seen a barbeque that size!   The backyard is a large size and is as well manicured as the front with Gerbera daisies, roses and greenery in a beautiful garden.

There are four washrooms, three mid-size bedrooms and a master suite. The master bedroom has two grand walk-in closets that would make any female swoon in delight. The feminine closet has an island in the centre with a built-in vanity and enough drawers to keep any woman's accessories organized and easy to find. It even gives my closet competition.

One of the bedrooms is designed to be a child's room but you can tell it has never been used. Exquisite crystal chandeliers and light fixtures set off an ambiance of beautiful light displays throughout the home. The only thing I can say is missing from this house is hints of Brandon's own personality. There is no artwork, pictures or colour on the walls.

After playing games with Angel, Brandon escapes into the kitchen for about ten minutes and then returns to lead Angel and me into his dining room. The table is set for two and I balance Angel on my right leg. He plays the roles of both server and feeder throughout the delicious five-course meal. Angel claps her hands every time he disappears into the kitchen and reappears with something new. We both laugh as she helps herself to the pasta by digging both of her tiny little hands into the dish and bringing a handful up into her mouth. There is tomato sauce and noodles everywhere. Thank goodness for easy-to-clean hardwood floors.

The meal is wonderful! Every time Brandon brings out the next dish, he seems so nervous about my reaction. I reassure him that everything tastes delectable. Only at the end of the meal does he admit he does not cook often and had to call his mom for crash courses during the preparation. It makes me feel so special that he went through all that trouble for me. Brandon is definitely worth keeping.

It is not long after we finish eating that all the excitement of the day tires out Angel and she goes down for a nap. We bring her upstairs to the child's room and go to the living room to spend some time together. Brandon dims the lights and turns on his electric fireplace, without the heat setting, as we lay on his plush rug. My head rests on Brandon's forearm and I am perfectly positioned to gaze into his big brown eyes. It is the perfect opportunity to tell him what is on my heart.

"Baby, there is something I need to talk to you about," I begin.

"What's up, sweetie?" he asks, unable to hide a hint of concern in his voice.

He tries to raise his body but I put a gentle hand on his shoulder to signal to him to stay as he is.

"I've been thinking about us and our relationship, and how far we've come right now and..."

"Aaron, please don't," he interrupts with a sense of urgency in his voice. "I know things are going fast and getting more serious than you want, but don't end things. I can slow down, or back off for a while but..."

"End things?" I am completely confused. "Brandon, I don't want things to end. I want things to get even better. I want you to spend more time with Angel and me. I want us to take our relationship to the next level."

I pause, not only to catch my breath but to fully take in this life-defining moment. I thank the universe and bask in the glory of my next stage in life. I am nervous about what I am about to say but I am one hundred percent confident in my decision.

"The most important thing Brandon is that I want you to stop paying me to be with me. I want to be with you freely. I want to be your girl." I hold my breath.

One look in Brandon's eyes, full of tears that escape and slide down his cheeks, are all I need to confirm that he is happy. He pulls me into the warmest embrace and covers my mouth with a kiss so breathtaking that I forget where I am. This is what love feels like. O-M-G! I realize in this very moment that I love him with everything I have.

"Aaron, I love you," Brandon whispers into my ear.

Talk about timing. Had he said those words just a few seconds before, he might have scared me off. He was right on time.

"I love you too Brandon," I say back, pressing my body against his and raising my head for another kiss.

We continue holding each other and exchanging kisses but Brandon does not try to make love to me. A little frustrated by this, I find the courage to confront him.

"Brandon, can I ask you something?"

"Sure baby, you can ask me anything."

"Um..., are you still attracted to me physically?" I blurt out.

"Of course I am, Aaron. Why would you ask me that?" He sounds puzzled.

"Well, since our fight, you haven't tried to sleep with me at all. I feel like...I mean, what's wrong?" I ask.

Brandon looks deeply into my eyes with so much emotion that I feel overwhelmed. He raises himself up to a sitting position and pulls me to sit against him as he wraps me in the most secure hug I have ever experienced. I feel so safe. I lean my head back onto his shoulder and he rests his chin on the top of my head.

"Aaron, believe me, I want you more now than I have ever wanted anyone in my entire life." he says as he turns me to face him, lifts my chin and looks into my eyes. "I want more from you than your body. I want all of you. I want to make you my wife.

You are worthy of so much more and I want to give you everything your heart desires. I long for you so much but I promised myself that the next time we slept together, it would be as man and wife, and I'm willing to wait for you because..." His lips graze my left cheek. "You are worth the wait."

We sit in silence as I bask in the wonders of his confession. Brandon wants me to be his...wife? No way. Never in a million years would I dream of this happening to me. I cannot help myself, I am experiencing verbal diarrhea and have to ask the most obvious question.

"Brandon," I whisper in a shaky voice, "why would you want to wife someone like me? I'm a prost-i-tute, a hoe. I sold my body and..."

"And what?" Brandon says in an authoritative voice. "Baby, no one is perfect. I can't judge you. After all, I was a client. That was just as bad. What I do know is how I feel about you and how you make me feel. Everyone deserves a happy life. I want to give you and Angel the life you deserve."

I wrap my arms around his neck and pull him in for another embrace. I do not want this moment to end...ever! I have been waiting for this for a long time.

Brandon and I begin to discuss plans for the future. He is concerned about me financially and I make it clear to him that I am walking away from the streets, period. We talk about things I could do, which include going back to school. When I tell him about my passion for decorating, he agrees that I had a natural talent. He is so supportive and encourages me to follow my heart and assures me he is going to help.

He tells me more about life with his ex-wife and I am shocked that anyone would ever cheat on someone like Brandon. Some people just do not know a good thing when they have it. Well, her loss was my gain! I decide to spend the night with Brandon since Angel is sleeping so well and we have shared such intimate moments.

"Hey, baby, maybe you can start your new career by helping me decorate this house. Tanika's style was minimalist and I haven't had a chance to do anything here. I've seen your place and would love it if you helped me," Brandon says.

Of course I agree and feel so excited about getting started. Brandon suggests we take before and after pictures to start building a portfolio for me. This man is perfect.

As we fall asleep in each other's arms in his king size four-poster bed, I think about the turn of events in my life. Nothing could ever make me go back to my old ways. The future is starting to look bright. I can finally see the pot of gold at the end of my rainbow. Forget the pot; I can finally see the rainbow!

Thirteen † Aaron

The last couple of weeks have flown by so quickly. It has been almost eight weeks since Brandon and I became official, and I am still floating on cloud nine. Everything has been happening so quickly for me, it is unbelievable. I have inherited the most foolish smile you can imagine and I am in no rush to get rid of it.

For starters, I practically live at his place and hardly ever go home. I started formulating my decorating concept for his home the day after our initial visit. We sat down and talked about everything from colours to artwork and music to get a sense of his style. Our conversation gave me a good starting point. Brandon also wanted me to include my personality into the design because he adores my style and wants me to feel at home. Even without him saying it, I know he wants me to move in soon. I will not object when asked.

The place has already taken on a new persona. Brandon invited some friends and colleagues over to see what I have done and I have been getting rave reviews from them. I have even booked other big jobs that will commence after I have completed this house. In the meantime, I have started a few small jobs on the side. Can you believe it? This is the best kind of busy I have ever been in my life. I have definitely found my niche and everything feels so simple.

Brandon recently sat me down to discuss something that matters a lot to him. He wanted to make sure that no matter how hectic our agendas become, we will always spend quality time with each other. We both gave our word. Since that conversation, we always sit down and have meals together. If I'm not at the house in time for dinner, Brandon refuses to go to bed without me. I love it!

As you and I both know, there is no such thing as a perfect world. There has to be something wrong—right? The only glitch in my life right now is that I have been blowing off Ruby. I guess I should not really say I am blowing her off but it probably seems that way to her. She seems very desperate to meet up with me for our girls' night, but I have been so busy with the house, Angel and Brandon that I have not had the time. I feel terrible.

Ruby has been the perfect friend, which only adds to my guilt. Something about her has changed, drastically. If she were being her usual rude self, it would be easier to not see her and blame it on her attitude. The few times I have had to speak with her, she listens patiently without interrupting as I ramble on about Brandon and my new career. I really thought she would laugh or make me feel stupid but she is so supportive. I want to say it almost seems fake, but that is just me being skeptical about things being too good in my life. I mean, really, it is a full three-sixty turn!

Ruby's most recent messages to meet up have become demanding. I really do not want to admit this, but her persistence is becoming a pain in my ass. In all due fairness, I have not seen her in over two months and I am being unreasonable. She just misses me, loves me and wants to be included in my new life. I promised myself that I would look through my schedule—yup, I have a schedule—and block some time out to spend with Ruby.

After all, was it not for Ruby who knows what would have happened to me. She rescued me from the cold, literally, and I owe her, big time. Some might say that if it was not for her, I might not have become a prostitute but then I probably would not have met Brandon. So overall, it was for the best because Brandon is so worth it!

I pull out my BlackBerry and search through my calendar to see what days I am free and find that I have a free weekend two weeks from today.

Perfect! I block off that Friday and Saturday, and send her a text message saying that is when I will be available. Almost immediately, I receive a reply. Wow! It is yet another change in Ruby since she normally takes hours to reply to a text message. With this situation taken care of I can now say my life is totally perfect!

A few hours later, I swing open the door to my favorite Benjamin Moore Paint store to pick up some paint chips. Lately, I have become close with the owners who give me discounts because I make so many paint orders and they want me to keep coming back.

"Hey, what's up, Larry? How are you today?" I say to the owner as I head over to the warm colour paint section.

I am working on a bachelor pad and the owner wants me to make his space more welcoming so any ladies who come by feel at home. Believe you me; he has a lot of ladies!

"I'm doing well, precious. Working on a new job?" he asks.

"Uh-huh, just another small one. A bachelor. He doesn't want the ladies to feel like they're in a sex pad, even though it is one." I giggle. "I'm going to give it a homey feel, so no sexy race car reds or get it on greens. You know what I mean?"

"Or...banging blues? I gotcha. Hey, come check out the new colour trend book that arrived today," he says.

He does not have to say another word. Picking out the paint chips would have to wait a minute. There is nothing like seeing the new colour forecasts. Hmmm, this salmon colour is a hot number. Mixed with a shade of deep grey, it would be a perfect combination to showcase both masculinity and femininity. I commit it to memory.

Forty minutes later, I leave the store armed with both paint chips and a few paint samples so I can show my client how lighting and location can affect colour. I have been going out of my way to ensure I do not get any negative feedback when I complete my jobs.

As I head into the parking lot, my phone starts going off.

"Hello?"

"Hey, sexy. It's your prince." Brandon says.

"My prince?" I tease playfully. "Denzel, is that you?"

"Ha, ha, little lady, very funny. Where you at?"

"I just left Larry's store. I'm working on your friend Dominick's place now. I was picking up paint chips to show him some colour ideas tomorrow."

"Hmm," Brandon replies. "I'm not too sure if I'm comfortable with you being alone with Dominick. He's quite the charmer, you know."

Although he is teasing, I can tell Brandon is a tad bit insecure.

"Baby, I only have eyes for one man and that's you. Believe that, sweetie," I respond with tenderness.

"Aww, I love you, baby. Oh yeah, before I forget, I wanted to let you know that I have tickets for a dinner and dance event sponsored by my company on the eighteenth. It's a black tie affair so it should be really nice," Brandon says.

"Oooh, Brandon that sounds great. Nice and classy. Let me just put that into my calendar."

I pull the phone away from my ear to mark the date in my calendar and realize it is the same date I saved for my weekend with Ruby.

"Aw, geez. Sorry baby, that's the weekend I just confirmed with Ruby. I'm going to have to pass," I relay with regret in my voice.

I feel bad and I would rather go with him to this event but the thought off putting off Ruby; yet again, sends chills up my spine. She has been patient so far but who knows what her breaking point is.

"Can't you postpone your plans...for me?" he pleads. "I really want to show you off and this is the perfect time."

It is so tempting but I know better. Now it is my turn to plead.

"Baby, I would if I could but I can't. After that weekend, I have no free time until three weeks later and I have put her off so much already. Please don't be mad."

"Okay, fair enough. I mean, I just found out about this event and sprung it on you kind of last minute. I guess I can share you for one weekend," he says.

This is why I adore this man. He is not only loving, charming and sexy, but he is also reasonable.

"Thanks, baby," I gush.

"No problem. Are you going to be on time for dinner tonight?"

"Definitely. See you soon, baby."

I slide into the brand new drop-top Mercedes Benz coupe with white exterior and interior that Brandon insisted on buying for me three weeks ago. He said the car suited me when we went on a vehicle hunt. I was actually going to buy an SUV or something more appropriate for a mommy but Brandon said he wanted only the best for me and I made the car look good. It still has that awesome new car smell that I absolutely adore. Thank goodness I only have one child because this is definitely not a family type of car. I love it and feel like the "it" girl when I am driving it. I even bought white Chanel glasses to match.

Tonight, Brandon is taking me to have dinner at 360 Restaurant, which sits atop the CN Tower and with all my daily tasks done, I head straight home to get ready. I already arranged with Carm to pick up Angel from daycare and stay overnight at my apartment. I am going back to the house with Brandon tonight.

Okay, confession time. There is one other thing that is making my perfect life not so perfect: the lack of lovemaking. I am one horny woman, to say the least, and Brandon will not budge on this promise for anything. The other day, I sat him down and told him he does not have anything to prove to me. I know he values me and understands my worth, and sex is not going to change that. He told me that he was doing it for him and he was looking forward to our honeymoon. This man is talking about our honeymoon and he has not even asked me to marry him yet.

I do feel different though. Brandon wanting to be around me so much without making love makes me feel good. Yes, I have to take many cold showers to calm myself but it is a small price to pay. I wish he would ask me to marry him already so I could at least do a countdown or something—I am just saying!

The fact that neither one of us has had sex since the last time we slept together makes me feel kind of like a virgin. Brandon was the only client whom I let do certain things to me in the first place. I would service my other clients in different ways and as often as possible, avoided having actual intercourse with them. Pleasuring them was still dirty, but not as dirty. So in my mind, I believe that I have not been defiled and I am worthy of wearing white when the time comes to walk down that aisle. There may be a hint of colour in the bustier portion of the dress, but that is it!

"You are worthy because you are beautifully and wonderfully made," says the voice.

Yes, the voice is still here. I actually smile because now the voice does not bother me. It does not feel as condescending now and I almost will it to speak to me. Crazy, right? That is how happy I am. Nothing upsets me these days.

Fourteen † Ruby

Ruby read and reread the text message Aaron sent her earlier that day. She still could not get over the audacity of her message. It read:

HEY GIRL. HAVE SOME FREE TIME 2 WKNDS FROM NOW. CAN HOOK UP FRI NGHT UNTIL SAT AFT. MAKE THE ARRANGEMENTS AND TEXT ME BACK A CONFIRMATION. SEE U SOON.—A

Who the hell does this girl think she is texting me as if I am one of her little decorating clients? Ruby thought back over the last two months when she had to bite her tongue and endure Aaron's endless chatter about Scar and colours and focal points and whatever else she rambled on about.

There was so many times during the conversation that she wanted to tell her to shut her mouth and stop being such a square head. The way she wrote 'MAKE THE ARRANGEMENTS' like Ruby was her personal assistant or something really bothered her. When did Aaron become the one who called the shots? That was Ruby's job and it was well earned. It took her years on the street to earn that power. All Aaron did was lay on her back; she did not do a damn thing to earn any kind of status! Ruby on the other hand had to fight, steal and cheat her way to the top. How dare that little heifer think she was better than Ruby?

Ruby only endured the constant chatter so she could keep Aaron thinking everything was good. If Aaron knew her the way she should have, she would have noticed Ruby's fraudulence. The little hussy was so wrapped in herself that she did not know her foot from her ass nowadays.

Ruby had actually been starting to have a change of heart regarding her plan to bring Aaron back to earth. When she thought of Aaron alone with these two men who were basically told to have their way with her, she felt remorse. Is this not the very reason she saved Aaron from the streets so many years ago, to protect her from these things? Now she was handing her over to them. It was that bloody text message that sent Ruby back over the edge. Aaron was biting the hand that fed her all these years and she could not let it happen that easily. No way! The girl practically replaced Ruby with Scar in the blink of an eye so why should Ruby worry about what happened to her? Why should she care?

It is not as if she had not been having sex with different men all these years. The only difference now was Scar was getting it for free. Is life not a bitch? Not only did Scar steal her best friend, he also totally manipulated Aaron in the process. Ruby entertained the idea of having Scar dealt with on the low. That man needed to be taught a lesson. He was lucky that she had to focus all her attention on Aaron right now.

Her plan was simple and the work of a genius if she did say so herself. She would meet Aaron at the room where the beautician and masseuse would be waiting. After they were pampered, she would tell Aaron that she had a special surprise for her but had forgotten it in the car. The two guys would go upstairs and demand that Aaron performs on them or else. She would automatically go into survival mode and service the guys, and it would bring her back to reality of who she was. They would give her a thousand dollars, which Ruby would have given them ahead of time, to remind her of what it was like to be paid for her goodies.

Ruby would go back upstairs, and Aaron would beg Ruby to forgive her and take her back to the streets. After slapping Aaron around to teach her a lesson, Ruby would welcome her back, but there would be new rules.

Aaron would have to earn back her status as Ruby's friend. Until then, she would be treated like all of Ruby's other *employees*. Ruby wanted a certain amount of money weekly from Aaron and Aaron would only keep a percentage of what she made. Aaron wanted a career and Ruby would give her a career. The plan was brilliant.

Ruby wished it did not have to come to this but she knew it was for Aaron's good. She still loved Aaron and knew the life she was living now was not really what she really wanted. Scar had brainwashed the girl and she needed tough love from Ruby.

Ruby sat back on her queen size bed and placed her hands behind her head in triumph. Lately, this spot served to soothe her constant bouts with depression. Yes, she thought to herself, everything was going to be all right. For the first time in months, she didn't need ice cream to feel good. She fell asleep as though she were a newborn baby wrapped in her mother's loving arms.

Fifteen † Brandon

Brandon and Aaron rode the elevator to the top of the CN Tower. He squeezed his eyes shut as the elevator climbed and climbed and climbed. Thank goodness the restaurant did not have those ridiculous glass floors through which you could see how high you really were and how much of a drop there was beneath you.

Brandon was afraid of heights but did not share this little fact with anyone. He hated being the butt of anyone's jokes or teasing, and he hated to show weakness. At a very young age, his father taught him that men, real men, had no fear. When he was a child and his father found out he was afraid of water, he took Brandon out on a fishing trip and threw him into the water. He did not pull him out until Brandon almost drowned. This lesson was repeated a few times until his father believed the fear was cured. If anything, it was actually escalated but Brandon knew better than to ever admit that to his father or there would be dire consequences.

Brandon knew all about dire consequences after he walked in on a physical fight between his parents during which his dad was putting a beating on his mom. Without a thought, he ran up to his dad and pushed him off her. When his dad turned to face him, the look in his eyes made Brandon regret what he had done. He turned and bolted out the room.

"You want to be a man, boy? Don't run. Stand and face me," his dad said but Brandon kept running.

A shove from behind him sent him flying into a glass table in the hallway that cut his back. His dad stepped over him and laughed at what a coward Brandon was.

Brandon had the awful scar on his back as a reminder of the day when he learned how to hide his fears, which was exactly what he did now. He chose the CN Tower because it was a perfect setting for a romantic evening and they were definitely overdue for one but Aaron would never know about his fear.

When they finally arrived at the top, they were quickly ushered to their reserved table. Everything about this restaurant was charming. The moving floors were a nice touch. He always thought that rotating floors would make him become dizzy but they did not. In fact, he hardly noticed. The servers were delightful and the food was excellent. He had a slow roasted, aged, Canadian AAA rib of beef with rosemary bread pudding, summer vegetables and natural jus. The meat was so tender and juicy. Topped off with a bottle of wine, he was good to go. He noticed that Aaron was a little giddy and could not take her eyes off of him.

Brandon was nervous beyond his imagination and it was not only because they were one thousand, one hundred and fifty one feet in the air. There was something even more important on his mind and the moment was here. The server made eye contact with him as he brought over their desserts on a silver platter topped with a dome-shaped cover. As the server revealed Aaron's dessert, Brandon went down on one knee. The server, as previously planned, was carrying, on his silver platter, the diamond engagement ring Aaron went crazy over in the jewellery store. She still did not know Brandon was in the store that day.

"Aaron," Brandon said in a soft but solid voice, "you are the love of my life and the sole owner of my heart. Nothing seems impossible when I'm with you. Aaron, my sweet angel, will you marry me?"

Aaron stared at the ring in awe. She looked overwhelmed, shocked and confused at the same time.

"Brandon, how could you have known...about this ring? I went back and it was...was...gone," Aaron stuttered as her eyes filled up with tears. "I was so...how could..."

"My love, will you marry me?" Brandon repeated gently and with purpose.

Aaron looked at Brandon with a new gleam in her eyes. The most dazzling smile took over her face.

"Yes, of course, yes! Yes, yes, yes!" Aaron shouted and jumped into Brandon's arms for a warm kiss and embrace.

Everyone within earshot applauded, including the manager who had come out to witness the well planned proposal.

The rest of the night was a beautiful hazy blur. After leaving the restaurant, Brandon drove for about an hour and took Aaron for a romantic walk down in Niagara Falls. He wanted the night to remain in her memories forever and had more wonderful surprises for her. As they walked arm in arm alongside the beautiful stretch of waterfall, Aaron shared with Brandon her vision for a perfect wedding.

She wanted a small intimate wedding, which would only include their families and true friends because she wanted to be able to look out and recognize everyone who came to celebrate their day. She dreamed of an elegant but simple dress with a long train. She could not wait to start hunting for the perfect matching dress for Angel and wondered if Angel was old enough to bear the responsibility of flower girl. She wanted white and yellow roses to adorn their reception hall. Brandon got the feeling that she was already rehearsing her wedding vows in her head but he knew with great certainty that the words would flow effortlessly.

Brandon was overjoyed as he listened intently to her wish list for her perfect day. He was impressed with how real and unselfish she was. Aaron was clearly not one of those "Bridezillas" he glimpsed a few times on television, asking for the sky and then some for their day. Her number one goal was intimacy and love. The bling and ching ching that many women wanted were not her priorities. He felt truly blessed that she accepted and was thankful that he had bought the ring after overhearing it was the one she had wanted. He wanted to live up to her expectations and become her knight in shining armour.

After walking and talking the night away, Brandon took Aaron back to the hotel where he had a suite reserved and set up with the hotel's romance package to complete their night. He wanted her to get used to receiving the best of the best from her future husband and it would start right now.

The beauty of the room that Brandon booked captivated Aaron. From the king size bed to the deep-soaking tub and a separate rainfall shower in the luxurious washroom, Brandon knew the night was going to be memorable. They popped a bottle of champagne that had been chilled and placed in the room for them and toasted to their future.

Naturally, kissing and groping soon came into play and after a few minutes, Aaron started to unbutton his pants. Brandon skillfully and respectively moved her hand away and continued exploring her lips with his but Aaron pulled away so she could look into his eyes.

"Baby, I want you so much right now. Don't stop me," she pleaded desperately.

Brandon pulled her into his arms as he pulled himself to rest against the headboard of the bed. He silently cursed himself for letting innocent kissing turn into hot and passionate touching and groping.

"Sweetie, I made a promise that I intend to keep. I want our life to start with keeping promises to each other. Can you understand that, baby? I need you to understand how important that is to me and how much I love you."

After a moment's hesitation, she sighed deeply. He could tell by her facial expression that his request was not an easy task.

"I understand, baby, I do." With a gentle laugh she added, "Let's get married as soon as possible because I don't know how long I can hold out!"

They both laughed and embraced, instantly lightening the mood. They resumed their discussion about the wedding and agreed that three months gave them plenty of time to inform their loved ones and prepare for their special day. Aaron was confident that she could handle all the arrangements for the church and the reception hall, and Brandon would take care of the legal aspect of the wedding. They definitely balanced each other out and looked forward to getting started.

That night, Brandon held on to her with all his might. He did not know why but he had a weird feeling that was a bit unsettling. It was the kind of feeling you get when you left for vacation and wondered if you set the security alarm for the house or turned off the iron. Something just did not feel right. Determined not to let anything, not even his mind, ruin this day, he brushed the feeling aside and cuddled Aaron even closer.

She turned, smiled up at him and shortly after fell into a deep slumber. Brandon was left staring at his future bride as he memorized every detail of her face and tried to discover anything new he may have missed before. His only discovery was a tiny dimple on her left cheek that was so small he would not have noticed it any other time. He lightly kissed the area and thanked God for sending Aaron to him.

Brandon was not a religious person but decided during college that having something to believe in was not such a bad thing. His college roommate had been very religious and a little pushy about his faith but he introduced Brandon to a God who was fun and full of love. Occasionally, Brandon still credited this God with any success he had or gift he received. Aaron was his greatest gift of all.

Brandon also could not wait to officially adopt Angel as his own little girl. He was glad she was young and would grow up knowing him as her father with no questions. He had amazing plans for her life and could not wait to wake up and see her beautiful little face every day. A trip to Disneyland topped his list of things to do with his little girl.

Brandon drifted off to sleep, peaceful and content. Neither Brandon nor Aaron could have predicted the awful fate that was lurking in the dark waiting to tear apart the bond that they worked so hard to create.

Sixteen † Ruby

Today was the day she would get Aaron back and Ruby was more than excited. She could hardly sleep the night before, trying to contain her joy. Everything was set and in place. Ruby dotted all of her I's and crossed every last T to ensure everything went smoothly. She left no room for error simply because she had no room. Everything had to work like a well-oiled machine for the plan to be a success.

Ruby longed to hold her best friend in her arms even though Aaron would have to suffer some well-deserved consequences before they could have everything go back to normal. As she lay in her bed the previous night fantasizing about today's events, she wondered if she should ease up a little bit on the length of time she intended to punish Aaron. She had planned to give the girl grief for at least six months before allowing her back into their tight friendship circle but was unsure if she could hold out so long. She really yearned to have things back to the way they used to be. She decided to go with the flow. If Aaron worked hard to prove herself worthy, she would lessen the time. She smiled at her *generosity*. She really did spoil the girl.

After being snapped back to reality by the familiar sound of her cell phone, Ruby checked the number and a quick flash of panic ran through her as she saw Aaron's number on the screen. What if Aaron was calling to cancel or to change the date? She crossed her fingers, took a deep breath and then answered her phone.

"What's up?" she said in her best casual tone, not wanting Aaron to detect any fear in her voice.

"Nothing, girl. I'm just calling to tell you I'm so excited about today! I miss you so much and have so much to tell you," Aaron said.

Ruby wanted to stick her finger down her throat to help release the bile she felt raising in her stomach but chose to give the type of response she knew Aaron wanted. It would not be long before the sickening stories, sappiness, and the nonsense ended forever.

"Me too, girl!" she said in a syrupy tone that matched the one Aaron had been using over the last couple of weeks. "I can't wait for you to fill me in on what else is going on in your life!"

"I know, right?" Aaron responded. "Who knew that you and I would get to this chapter in our lives? Anyways, I have a few errands to run before our date so I'll see you soon. Bye!"

"Bye!" Ruby echoed and then hung up.

This frigging girl was so self-centered now. All she wanted to do was talk about herself. Ruby could only imagine the bullshit she wanted to share with her now. She probably got Scar's name tattooed across her ass or on her forehead or something. It was funny that in the last few months Aaron never once asked Ruby about her life. Every conversation had to do with her new career or romance with Scar. Ruby felt the familiar anger and hurt feeling rising in the pit of her belly, and willed it to go away with happier thoughts of what the day held. It is almost over, she thought to herself. This so-called new chapter of their lives was about to change. From here on out, there would be a new writer for this story. She was taking on the role of author and publisher of the events of their lives. Aaron would be at the mercy of Ruby's pen strokes and the chapters that were to come were definitely not the kind you read in fairy tales. The happy ending would belong to Ruby and she planned to make sure of it—no matter what it took. You had better believe that.

Seventeen † Aaron

I really have to learn to control and contain my happiness. People are actually moving out of my way as I walk up the aisle in the grocery store with the world's biggest grin on my face. Until recently, I didn't realize how uncomfortable friendliness makes strangers feel sometimes. I cannot help myself though, I feel like I love everyone and everything and I stare at other happy couples anywhere I go. I never really noticed them before but now it's like we belong in the same club. Every time I pass a couple, I want congratulate them and swap tales of happiness. I know it's corny but I cannot help how I feel and I do not care what anyone else; except Brandon, thinks. Life is so amazing and now I understand that before I fell in love with Brandon, I was only surviving and not living. Now I am truly alive!

Since I will be gone on my girls' night with Ruby until tomorrow and Brandon volunteered to take Angel for the day, I have decided to get all her favourite foods and leave them. Carm will be coming to baby-sit tomorrow afternoon so Brandon can go to his work event. She has also already agreed to stay on as my sitter even though my apartment is on the market and we will be living at Brandon's, because I have arranged transportation back and forth to the house. I am happy I do not have to lose her because Carm is such an important person in our life. I plan to ask her to be my bridesmaid and Ruby to be my maid of honour. A small wedding party fits perfectly into my plan to have an intimate celebration.

After walking and tossing things into my cart without a thought, by the time I get to the check out, I look down to find it filled to the top. I do not even remember picking up most of the things. Oh well, Brandon and I go through food quickly. Now that there is another adult in my life, I do not have to worry about buying too much and throwing things out. Brandon has the appetite of a scavenger and I love it! After we are married, I plan to take some cooking classes to increase my menu selection. Right now, pasta is my specialty but I want to be able to keep our dinner table exciting and fresh, and feed my family home cooked meals. I want to be that kind of wife. My mother was not a good cook and it really annoyed my father, but she did not care.

Two hundred dollars later, I head over to Brandon's house. He already has Angel and time is running out before I have to head downtown to meet Ruby. I pull into the driveway and make the necessary trips back and forth from the car to the front door to transfer the groceries. After my last run, I use the key Brandon recently gave me (how exciting!) to let myself in and announce my presence.

"Baby, I'm home!" I shout at the top of my lungs.

The familiar happy bubbles that swim through my body every time I come through the front door appear right on cue. Even though this house is so familiar to me, I still feel incredible every time I step over the threshold.

Brandon walks out of the kitchen, holding Angel on his hip. She has her Dora plush doll in her arms.

"Hey, gorgeous," he says, looking over my shoulder at the grocery bags. "Expecting a famine?" He grins.

"Ha, ha," I reply as I walk over to him and plant a kiss on his soft cheek and then one on Angel's. "Very funny!"

I repeat my transfer of grocery bags from the front door to the kitchen. Brandon leans against the counter embracing Angel and watching as I put things away. I am very aware of his stare and actually feel grateful for it. I love when he ogles me, even though his lazy butt should be helping.

When I finish unloading the last bag, Brandon takes my hand, guides me into the living room area and sits me down in our favourite loveseat. I can tell there is something on his mind. He puts Angel to sit on the floor, which is covered in *Dora the Explorer* merchandise.

"I've been thinking," he begins, "I really don't think it's a good idea for you to go to your girls' night."

"Oh come on Brandon, don't start this again!" I say.

We have had this discussion a few times in the last couple of days, and each time I had to assure Brandon that Ruby understands everything is different now.

"Baby, hear me out before you say anything," he says. "Lately, I have been having bad feelings that I can't explain about this night out. I know you think I am paranoid but I chalk it all up to intuition. I know Ruby is your friend but she is also a connection to a lifestyle you are no longer a part of. Maybe it's better to cut all ties and move on."

I know Brandon means well but I definitely have to let him know from now that I am a grown woman who is capable of making her own decisions and picking her own friends. There is no way I am going to be one of those women who has her husband telling her what to do.

"Brandon, I really don't want to have this conversation again;" I cut him short, hoping to convey my message without offending him. "We discussed this and I'm going. I need to think about Ruby's feelings too. She has been patient enough. There is absolutely nothing for you to worry about."

Brandon seems to hesitate slightly before speaking again.

"I am in no way trying to tell you what to do Aaron but I need to share how I feel. Maybe if I come with you, I can just make sure everything is okay."

I smile at Brandon but say nothing, understanding that he is just being protective because he loves me. But I definitely do not need a chaperone and do not feel Ruby would be pleased to have an intruder on our day, even if it was only for a little while. I really want her and Brandon to get along; an invasion would definitely rub her the wrong way.

I get up, walk over to him and kiss him fervently on the lips. I express my love with a tight squeeze, pull away and stare intently into his warm, brown eyes.

"I love you, Brandon and I'll see you tomorrow."

His shoulders sag briefly with defeat as he realizes I am going—without him.

"I love you too, baby. Be careful," he says.

I bend down to kiss my little girl good-bye, who is so busy she does not even stop to look up at me, then I head straight to the door and open it to leave. I do not know if it is the feeling of defiance towards my future husband or something else but when I step outside, something in the back of my mind is telling me not to go. The feeling actually overwhelms me and for a split second, I almost change my mind and turn back around. I am immediately reminded by my conscience of how much planning Ruby put into this night, and how unfair it would be to cancel. I will go and before Brandon knows it, I will be back, unharmed, in his arms.

"Listen to love," says the voice in my head.

Huh? What? Listen to love? What the heck does that mean? I try to convince myself that 'listen to love' means my love for Ruby, not Brandon. And the voice is not the be all and end all in my decision-making.

As I am driving downtown, bopping my head to the music on the local urban station, I start to relax and I find myself actually looking forward to spending time with Ruby. I vow to do it often, and then begin to rehearse out loud how I will approach the topic of my wedding and her role as my maid of honour.

"So, Ruby, the funniest thing happened. You know how you always thought weddings were the end of people's lives and you wouldn't be caught dead attending one? Well, I'm getting married and want you to be my maid of honour."

Nah. That sounds so wishy-washy. I will just wait until we are relaxed and comfortable then slip it in.

Forty-five minutes later, I give my car keys to the hotel valet and make my way up to the room number that Ruby texted to me. When I arrive at the top floor, I realize Ruby booked a honeymoon style suite and really went out of her way for our night. I knock on the door and within seconds, Ruby flings it open and wraps me in a bear hug.

"Hey, beyotch. I'm so glad you came!" she shouts as she pulls me inside. "We are going to have so much fun."

Again, that overwhelming feeling I had almost an hour ago as I stood outside of Brandon's house comes back but I quickly shake it off. I mean, what could I do now? Leave Ruby high and dry after all the thought she put into this?

"Girl, I'm happy I came too." I spot a bottle of something on the round table in the seating area of the room. "I'm going to have a drink." Then silently add, I really need something to calm my nerves.

This room is the crème de la crème of rooms. I thought the suite Brandon got the night he proposed was nice but this room is fit for a king. It reminds me of an updated version of the room in the movie, *Pretty Woman*. It is the type of suite someone could actually live in with its inset bedroom and a sunken living room area.

It does not take long before we are back in the old familiar routine of jokes and laughter. Ruby updates me on what some of our old friends are up to and I am not shocked that nothing has really changed. Everyone I left on the corner is still on the corner but this is the normal routine of street life. People usually only leave because of jail or death. Inwardly, I beam at my lucky fate. I was able to leave by another, much more pleasant, route.

An hour later, a masseuse and a woman who specializes in manicures and pedicures arrive. We change into knee-length, plush white robes and I lay on the mobile table that has been assembled in the room. I am the first to receive a full-body massage and I feel tension leave my body that I did not know I had—including the sexual tension I have carried for so long. How can something so painful feel so damn good? My body vibrates as the masseuse does a karate chop-like motion from the back of my ankles to my upper back. I turn and smile at Ruby, who has her feet in a portable foot spa while she is getting a manicure, then mouth the words "thank you." For a moment, Ruby's face drops into a stony gaze that sends chills up my spine, but her expression is quickly replaced with a smile. Ruby must have been deep in thought about something else.

Shortly after, we switch places and my feet feel so good in the foot spa, which is filled with fresh water and a drop of lavender oil that fills my nostrils with an inviting scent. My nails are long overdue for a manicure, and I love the way they have been shaped and how they glisten. Growing up, I always adored my hands and received so many compliments about the length of my fingers. The manicure only accentuates their beauty. I am certain Brandon will love it.

Dang! I promised myself that I would focus on Ruby and not allow Brandon to enter into my mind but I cannot help it. Thoughts of Brandon make me anxious to speed up this fun night so I can get back to him and Angel but I am determined to enjoy my time. With my schedule and wedding planning duties, I do not know when I will be available to have another night out with Ruby so I want to make the most of this one.

After our pampering is finished and everybody is gone, I follow Ruby to the bedroom and lay out on the elaborate bed. I feel as if this is the perfect moment to share my news. I turn over to face her with a sheepish grin.

"I have something to tell you."

With Ruby staring at me so attentively, I feel a bit intimidated and hesitant as all too familiar memories of her power begins to surface. I swiftly brush them away, remembering that my life is now changed and I no longer have to submit to Ruby's authority. With a new wave of courage, I flash my ring finger in Ruby's direction and turn the ring over so she can see the diamond since I had it hidden when I arrived. Then I announce:

"I'm getting married." And with a bought of verbal diarrhea, add, "And I want you to be my maid of honour."

I hold my breath as Ruby holds my left hand and stares intently at the ring.

"Isn't this the ring from the store?" she asks.

"Yes. Can you believe it? I still don't know how he knew that's the ring I wanted but it's the one he gave me." After a moment, a thought occurs to me. "Hey...did you tell Brandon about this ring?" I ask with hope in my voice.

O-M-G, it would make so much sense if she told him, and it would only be more perfect if Ruby already knew about the wedding and was excited about it.

"Hell nah. I didn't tell Scar shit," Ruby says jumping off the bed and almost knocking over the cute little side table.

She turns her back to me, staring out the window. Even without seeing her face, I feel a weird negative energy seeping from her pores. There is almost heat evaporating from her body and I feel the air in the room getting thick. A feeling of fear starts to overtake me and I instantly sit up with my back pressed into the headboard, bracing myself for whatever is to come.

When Ruby finally turns around to face me, she has the prettiest smile on her face.

"Girl, you know I am not into weddings and that entire smack but I am so happy for you!" She jumps on the bed and pulls me into a warm embrace.

My body instantly relaxes. I do not know what happened a second ago but I think it was my diffidence playing tricks on my mind. Ruby is showing me nothing but love.

"You don't know how happy I am to hear you say this," I reply still hugging her. "I was worried about how you would take it! So this means you'll be my maid of honour?"

"Of course I will be your maid of honour, Aaron. I wouldn't have it any other way!" she gushes.

I nearly burst with excitement, telling Ruby how Brandon proposed and how engaged life has been. She is so quiet and still, intensely absorbing everything I say. Then she smiles oddly and someone who doesn't know Ruby would probably think it was scary, but I know that is happiness plastered all over her face. My love for Ruby keeps escalating. Even though my life is changing so quickly and dramatically, she is willing to swallow her pride and terminate her own rules so she can participate in my wedding. I am the luckiest girl in the world.

After I finish talking, Ruby hugs and congratulates me again. She then reveals she has a surprise for me that is perfect for the occasion but has to retrieve it from her car. As she gets dressed, she tells me not to bother changing out of the robe. Our night of pampering is definitely not over and she will change back into hers when she returns.

After Ruby leaves, I lie back on the bed and let out a deep relaxed breath. I knew Brandon had nothing to worry about and I cannot wait until tomorrow to let him know how very wrong he was. I close my eyes and allow any negative energy to escape my body as I let my mind drift to thoughts of the future. It is not long before my eyelids get heavy and thoughts of Brandon take over.

In my dream, Brandon is standing at the front of a church, strong and handsome, waiting for me with patience and tenderness in his eyes. As a beautiful melody plays over the speakers, I float gracefully down the aisle towards the love of my life. My white dress flows around me angelically as I step over the carefully placed white rose petals that Angel dropped on the floor moments before. All eyes are on me but the only person I see is Brandon and it seems like forever before I join him at the altar. He reaches for my hand as I step to face him.

"My love," he whispers, "thank you for being the beat in my heart and the blood that flows through my veins. You are my everything and I absolutely adore you. You are my perfection in an imperfect world. You are the reason I am on this earth. I was made for you and you for me. With you, I have discovered and live the meaning of love, and cannot wait to spend the rest of my life with you. With you, I have found love because you are love. You are my most precious reward in life and I will cherish you for always." He slips the ring on my finger.

"My heart," I whisper, blinking back tears that are fighting to flow from my eyes, "I am thankful for the day you walked into my life and claimed me as your girl. My life before now no longer matters and I look forward to everything life with you has to offer. You blot out any tragedies from my past and give me a second chance at a life—a real life. You are the man of my dreams, my Prince Charming. Love came to me so intensely with you and I seek nothing but your touch. I want to share the rest of my life with you and promise to be everything you will ever need—your love, heart, and best friend."

I slip the ring on his finger and we embrace, exchanging the most passionate kiss I ever had.

We now glide together on the dance floor to romantic songs, holding each other closely, moving as one and filling the room with passion and unconditional love. Our hearts beat rhythmically together and I am so very much alive! Brandon kisses me from the top of my head to the nape of my neck, not caring who is witnessing our act of love. We whirl and whirl to the music.

Brandon now lays me on the centre of a bed covered with the softest white silk sheets that feel like butter underneath my back. I still have on my wedding dress and hold perfectly still in anticipation of becoming one with Brandon. He rushes nothing as he slowly peels off my dress, sheer stockings and undergarments and then takes his time getting to know every inch of my body again. It is like the first time for both of us. My body arches and moves at the feel of his lips. Tiny kisses trail up and down my legs, and Brandon mumbles words of appreciation as he savours my smooth, silky skin. Every cell in my body applauds with respect and yearning. My fingers make their way into his hair and I cannot help the tugging I inflict as I wait patiently through this anticipation, which feels like torture. I want him now and I want him more than anything else in the world.

Suddenly, my head slams hard against the headboard. As I try to look at Brandon to see what is wrong, I am met with a hard slap across my face as the soft music that was playing in the background becomes louder.

"Whore!" I hear him shout.

"What?" I say as my eyes fly open and I am torn out of my sleep.

I am frozen in fear as two men I do not recognize stand over the bed.

"Who...what...what the?" I stutter.

"Shut up, whore, and don't ask any questions," says the bigger man as he starts to unbuckle his belt.

His intent is clear and I do not know what to think or do. Groggy with sleep, it takes me a moment to remember where I am. Then it comes back to me— Ruby, girls' night, hotel room.

"How did you get in here?" I demand before I scream out for Ruby.

My head flies sideways as sharp pain inflames my face and I feel the blood rush from my mouth. I whimper as the man drags me towards him by my legs and positions me directly beneath him. The other guy pries my legs apart as I do my best to use my leg muscles to keep them together.

"What are you doing?" I scream. "Stop!"

My words are muffled as the big guy covers my face with sloppy wet kisses that make me want to gag. I try with all my might to fight him off but I am quickly overpowered by the two of them. I refuse to lose the fight. I have to protect my body not only for myself, but also for Brandon.

"Whore, you're going to do what you were paid to do even if we have to kill you to get it, understand?" the man whispers to me in between kissing my face and pulling away my robe. "We heard you are the best and we both want a piece of you, so start enjoying it. We are going to have ourselves a wonderful night. We have you all night, sweetie, and you can thank your friend for that."

As the word *friend* leaves his lips and he forcefully enters my body, every bit of my dignity and self-worth dissolve. Time seems to stand still at the apprehension of what is taking place. I have lost the fight.

Tears pour down my face with the realization that all of my dreams are shattered. My short-lived fantasy world ceases to exist. With every thrust, grunt and groan, I am reminded of who I truly am and how much of a joke these last couples of months of my life have really been. My mind drifts back to Brandon. Oh, sweet Brandon. What a joke I will be to him now. I almost laugh at the irony of the situation. Here he is, saving himself for me and here I am, a dirty whore being ravaged by two strangers. Brandon thought I was his fiancé and future wife. Hell no. I was his hired call girl playing dress-up. How dare he think he could make a whore into a housewife? *How dare he*?

I give up entirely and leave my body behind to these thugs, as they pass me back and forth throughout the night. I am an empty shell with no soul. I am dead to the world.

I drift off to a place of pure blackness as the pain becomes too much to bear. I am stuck but see Brandon and Angel ahead of me, shining like a light. I watch them playing together, enjoying their bond but when I try to get close to them, they turn and walk away. I call out to them, but no matter how much I scream, I have no voice. Angel does not even look at me. It is like she knows I am there but chooses not to acknowledge my existence. Brandon, on the other hand, looks directly at me and shakes his head. I hear his thoughts, sharp as razor blades and accusing. He has sacrificed so much for me—his reputation, dignity and trust—for nothing. There is so much disgust in his eyes. He whispers something to Angel and she finally looks at me, dead-on. At once, they both break out into hysterical laughter. The more they laugh, the more my body shatters, one bone at a time, until I am nothing but dirt.

Angel knows her mom is a whore. The dirty little secret I tried to hide from her is out. I can see in her eyes that she thinks I am unworthy and is ashamed. I accept that she has a right to feel this way. I always knew the time would come when I had to face the music. The time is now.

Eighteen † Ruby

It was early Saturday morning as Ruby rode the elevator to go back to the suite so she could comfort and then bully Aaron as planned. There were moments the day before when she almost wanted to cancel her plan but was glad she did not. Aaron was being sucked into a world in which she did not belong and Ruby knew she had to step in to save her best friend's life. Still, she was having second thoughts about her plan until Aaron announced she was getting married.

Aaron was in over her head and quickly sinking. This girl was so far gone that she thought Ruby would be her maid of honour and actually suggested that Ruby had clued in Scar about the ring. The girl was mad. It was a mystery to Ruby how he could have known about the ring but she did not care either way. It was probably just luck. As Aaron was blabbing on incessantly about Scar, Ruby stopped having any doubts about her scheme. Not only did she plan to go ahead with it, Ruby realized she also needed to step it up.

As she left her building, Ruby started to remember how she felt empowered when she left the room and the two thugs met her in the lobby. She handed them the keys and whispered to G, "No mercy." Those words were her code phrase for the thugs to go as far as they needed to remind Aaron she was a whore and at their mercy all night. At first, she only planned to leave them alone with Aaron for only a couple of hours, but she knew what needed to be done. Angel needed her mom to be real again and Ruby needed her friend.

Although she tossed and turned with guilt all night, she was comforted with thoughts of plans for the future. After last night, Ruby would not need to treat Aaron badly for six months. She knew that Aaron would behave exactly as required.

After arriving at the hotel, Ruby felt a cold chill go up her spine as she stepped onto the top floor. She paused and cautiously looked around. When nothing seemed out of place, she proceeded down the hallway to the room. Using her room key, Ruby let herself in, expecting to hear or see Aaron moving around. Instead, she was greeted with silence.

"Aaron?" Ruby called out but was met with more silence.

Odd. Had Aaron left before Ruby came back? This was not part of her plan. Ruby walked around the living room area of the suite and checked the washroom to see if there was evidence that Aaron had showered before she left. Knowing Aaron and her routine, she would have taken a long hot shower to wash away the evidence of a night full of pleasure. It was unnerving that nothing was out of place. It was as though Aaron never came into the bathroom at all.

Ruby's footsteps slowed as she walked towards the closed bedroom door. A feeling made its way through her body and she recognized it as the same one she felt the morning she discovered her baby sister's lifeless body. She was afraid of what was on the other side of the door but she had to know. No—she was being crazy and told herself to calm down. Aaron was okay. She had just checked out. With a renewed confidence, Ruby swung open the door and an unnatural scream escaped her lips.

Aaron's naked body lay lifeless on the bed, covered in streaks of blood. Her eyes were swollen shut and blackened with bruises. She lay so still that Ruby knew she was dead. Aside from bruises, her body had traces of teeth marks and there were empty condom packets all over the room.

"Help me! Somebody help me!" Ruby cried out in terror. "Please!"

She ran out of the suite, screaming and banging on every door in sight.

Nineteen † Brandon

"God, please, if you can hear me, let Aaron be alright."

This chant had become a continuous prayer from Brandon since he got the phone call from a paramedic who had gotten his name out of Aaron's phone and called to let him know she had been taken to the hospital. Brandon raced to the downtown hospital at top speed with complete disregard for the speed limits he was breaking or the amount of cars he was cutting off or tailgating. He could hardly remember how he got to the hospital when he pulled into the parking lot.

Brandon rushed inside and straight up to the floor and room he was given on the phone. In the room, a nurse was looking at Aaron's charts and her friend Ruby was in the corner trembling. He had no words for this parasite and he knew that she was somehow connected to what happened to Aaron. His heart stopped as he stared at his once beautiful energetic fiancé who was lying on the hospital bed. Her eyes were black and blue, and swollen shut. He could also see bruises all over her neck, and what looked like teeth marks. He forced himself to move his eyes away as anger started to build deep in his soul.

He gently took Aaron's frail hands into his. Her hands seemed to be the only recognizable part of her beauty right now as they remained soft to the touch. They were a reminder of who she really was.

"Aaron, my sweet Aaron," he whispered softly into her ear as he gently stroked her hands with his thumbs.

She did not move—not even a twitch. A tear slowly fell from his eye and rolled down his cheek.

He looked up at Ruby, who seemed to be in a state of shock. He was surprised that she was cowering in the corner so far away from the bed. She was a far cry from the butch girl who he saw Aaron with at the mall the day he purchased her engagement ring. As much as he did not want to talk to Ruby, she was the only source of information.

"What happened?" he managed to ask, but received no response.

Ruby seemed to be on another planet as she stared through him.

"She...he...," she stammered before withdrawing back into her world.

Brandon realized that she was not going to be any help to him right now. The nurse who had reviewing Aaron's charts when Brandon arrived returned.

"Can you please tell me what the hell happened?" he frantically said to her.

She looked at him as though seeing him for the first time.

"Oh," she said, "are you related to the patient?"

"This is my fiancé and I want to know what happened!" he shouted a little too aggressively.

Taken aback, the nurse quickly left the room, and returned with a security guard and the doctor. The doctor walked over and extended his hand.

"I am Dr. Kraus, and I am looking after your fiancé." He glanced over at Ruby and then said to Brandon, "Do you mind stepping outside to discuss her condition?"

Brandon followed him and was updated on Aaron's injuries. Without knowing the details of how it actually happened, the doctor told Brandon that Aaron had been repeatedly raped and assaulted, and was heavily sedated right now. She had come to a couple of times but became so hysterical that they had to continually administer drugs to keep her calm. She suffered severe tearing and bruising but her condition was not critical. Brandon silently sent God prayers of thanks for that. The doctor also explained that the police would need to speak with him. They were already at the hospital trying to get information from Ruby but she was in a mild state of shock and the doctor was keeping an eye on her to see if she had to be admitted as well.

It was not long before two uniformed police officers arrived and Brandon went down the hall with them into a quiet room where he could answer questions in private. They informed him that because Ruby was not forthcoming with any information, they needed to piece together the events of the night. Brandon shared with them everything he could think of leading up to when Aaron left the house. The information he gave could only place Ruby at the scene but did not offer any clues as to what actually transpired. He also told them that he had a bad feeling about Aaron and Ruby's girls' night but could not explain why. He did not want to tell the police officers that Aaron had been a prostitute and that Ruby was a part of that circle because he would then have to explain that he had been a client and everything would become even more complex.

Brandon knew that if he wanted to find out what truly happened, the information would need to come from Ruby. He silently cursed himself again for not listening to his instincts and keeping Aaron home. He did not want to come across as a bossy fiancé but now realized that would have been a small price to pay for her safety. Although he vowed to trust his gut from now on, that did not help Aaron right now. He already failed to protect her. He knew he should have gone with her and scoped out the scene. His plan had been to randomly visit her later in the night to make sure she was okay. Why had he not followed through? He hoped Aaron would forgive him for not being there to protect her. When he got his hands on whoever did this to her, they were going to wish the police had found them first.

He made such a fuss about not sleeping with her until they were married and now someone violated the innocence she had worked so hard to build over the past few months. She had wanted him to make love to her so badly and now he wished he had. The memories of her rape might make her not want to be touched again for a long time but he was willing to wait for her to heal. He would not rush her.

Brandon made up his mind to marry Aaron as soon as she was fit to leave the hospital and protect her the way he should have. He even contemplated selling the house, and moving her and Angel far away so they could start a new life in another province. He would discuss of all these things with Aaron when she was able to communicate. He loved her so much and seeing her like this was heart wrenching.

When he got back to the room, Ruby and the nurse were gone. He sat down beside Aaron's bed again and started talking to her.

"Hi, baby, it's me. I want you to know that you're safe now and I'll never let anyone hurt you ever again."

He laid his head beside her on the bed and wept silently. He could only imagine what was going through her mind when she was attacked.

An hour later Aaron began to stir. Brandon jumped up from the chair across the room in which he had gone to sit and rushed back to her side. She mumbled a few unclear words as she fought to open her eyes, which were so swollen that she was only able to open them a crack. It was evident the painkillers were still working because she looked dazed. It did not take long, however, for her to focus her blood shot eyes on Brandon.

"Hi, baby. It's me, Brandon," he said gently.

She stared at him, emotionless. It was as though she did not know who he was. Brandon did not allow this to offend him.

"Aaron, I just want you to know I'm here now and I won't leave your side," Brandon said, almost willing her to acknowledge him.

"Go away," she managed in a raspy voice. "Leave."

He could see that it was a major struggle for her to talk. She slowly turned her head so she did not have to look at him. Brandon held back his surprise. He knew she would be upset but he really did not expect her to reject him. He tried to comfort her again.

"Sweetheart, I know you're upset. I'm upset too. Let me be here for you, baby. Let me take care of you. I love you," he said.

Without any warning, Aaron let out a raspy scream as she flailed her arms and legs, fighting an invisible enemy. Having heard the commotion, the on-duty nurse came rushing in to see what was wrong. When she saw Aaron, she ran over to the bed and pressed the nurse-call button. The more she tried to calm Aaron down as she waited for help to arrive, the louder Aaron became. Eventually, two more nurses and a doctor came rushing in to help subdue Aaron as she repeated for Brandon to get out over and over. One of the nurses finally asked him to leave.

"I'm her fiancé!" he exclaimed but was still ushered out, and the room door was closed and locked behind him.

Brandon did not know what to do or think, as the sound of the lock seemed to explode in his ear. He leaned against the wall and slowly sunk to the floor into a pool of grief. Minutes felt like hours before the door opened and the extra nurses left the room. They walked quickly past Brandon, avoiding eye contact.

The doctor appeared a little while later and asked Brandon if he could speak with him. His eyes were soft and kind as he explained that Aaron asked them not to let Brandon come back and they had to respect her wishes. Even though Brandon was her fiancé, there was nothing they could do about it.

She became so hysterical they had to administer more drugs to sedate her and they could not afford to let her lose control again. She was in a very sensitive state and they needed to keep her calm so she could heal. The doctor also explained to Brandon that a traumatic experience like this often made the victim act out in unpredictable ways and although he could not make any promises, he was sure in time she would allow Brandon to visit.

Brandon left the hospital dumbfounded and lost. He had no one to turn to and talk about the situation. The other problem was Angel. What was he supposed do about her? He was more than willing to keep Angel with him and would find out from Carm what her schedule was like. But if Aaron did not want to see him, how would she feel about him watching her daughter? Everything was so complicated right now.

After arriving home, Brandon arranged with his company to work from home for two weeks so he could take care of Angel until he got word of what his next move should be. He loved Angel and refused to give her to anyone else while her mommy was recovering.

Brandon called the hospital daily to check on Aaron's progress. After a few days, he was told the outbursts of hysteria had ceased and she no longer needed to be sedated. He asked if he would be able to visit but was advised that she still did not want to see him.

When two weeks passed and there was still no word, he took a short-term leave of absence from work. He had plenty of vacation days and his seniority in the company ensured that the time away would not be a problem. He did not know what to do, whether he was coming or going and became a walking, talking nervous wreck but waited patiently to hear positive affirmation about Aaron. The only joy he felt came from Angel. He grew to love her even more as she became increasingly dependent on him. She was a wonderful little girl and although she asked for her mommy daily, she did not fuss or cry at night anymore. She really lived up to her name.

It was almost five weeks later when he finally got the call.

"It's me," Aaron said in a voice that contained absolutely no emotion. "I am home and would appreciate it if you brought Angel to Carm's place. I have arranged with her to bring Angel home. I want her home with me as soon as possible."

Brandon was shocked by her tone and continuous lack of emotion towards him.

"Aaron, what do you mean bring her to Carm's? Why am I not allowed to bring her over? I want to see you! I miss you. Let me bring her home so we can talk," Brandon pleaded.

"No!" she shouted. "I don't want to see you...ever! Bring my child to Carm's right now."

Brandon could not believe what she was saying. Why did she have so much anger towards him? How could she never want to see him again? They were engaged to be married.

"Baby, I know you are still upset and probably still in shock, but please, please don't push me away. I love you, you love me and we can get through this together. Aaron, please, don't do this!" Brandon cried into the phone.

"Brandon, listen to me and listen to me good. I'm going to tell you this one time and one time only. I do not want to see you anymore. I do not want to marry you. I am done. All I want is my baby back." Her voice was as cold as ice. "Thanks for watching her for me. Now, return Angel before I call the police and have you arrested for child abduction. She better be at Carm's house in an hour or I'm calling them!"

The line went dead. Brandon could not believe what was happening. She threatened him with the police and he knew she was not kidding. She broke off their engagement and tossed him aside like a piece of garbage. He was not only shocked but also terribly hurt by everything she said. It was as though he meant nothing to her.

With tears in his eyes, Brandon moved robotically around the house gathering Angel's things and getting her dressed to go to Carm's house. He felt like a deflated balloon and wondered what he must have done wrong in his lifetime to deserve this kind of fate. This is the hand that God dealt him. Was he that bad a person? Was this karma for something of which he was not aware?

When he dropped Angel off at Carmen's, he could not help but cry at the sight of her familiar face as she pulled him in for a big hug.

"Brandon, I'm so, so sorry. Don't worry. She'll come around. She is just in a lot of pain, give her time to heal. She is not in a good place right now," Carmen said.

He nodded silently and smiled at Carm. Brandon found comfort in her words. He could see that she was just as confused by Aaron's reaction towards him as he was.

He bent down, kissed Angel good-bye, quickly turned on his heels and walked away. He could not bear to look back at his little girl and know that he may never see her again.

How was it even possible to gain and lose two angels in one lifetime? How would he ever survive without them?

Twenty † Ruby

It had been five weeks since the plot to win back Aaron went so terribly wrong and Ruby had spent a lot of time reviewing why it had not worked. By now, they should have been back to their normal routine and enjoying the life Ruby carved out for them. But after that day, Aaron refused to speak with her. It had taken Ruby a few days to get over the initial shock of the whole incident and the weeks that followed had been so traumatizing she had to get medication from her doctor just to sleep. Then the bloody police called her down to 52 Division and questioned her about the night for over three hours. Ruby was more than familiar with how police officers worked because her rap sheet was long. She kept her answers the same, no matter how they tried to wear her down.

"No, I have no idea who could have done this."

"I wasn't in the room when it happened, so I can't identify who attacked her."

"I have no clue if she had any enemies."

"She's my friend. Why on earth would I be involved?"

"We planned a girls' night and I had to leave because I ate something and felt sick. Maybe she called someone to come over after I left."

"I have no idea about her personal life."

"Like I said before, I have no idea who could have done this."

"I want the person arrested even more than you do. She is my friend!"

"I told you, I wasn't in the room so I can't tell you who did it."

"I ate something bad and started having diarrhea. I just wanted to be home in my own bed."

"We don't talk about those kinds of things. I have no idea who she was sleeping with."

"To my knowledge, she had no enemies but I'm not with her 24/7."

Out of guilt, Ruby had made a few phone calls after the incident and had both of the thugs— dealt with. Even though she gave them permission to have no mercy on Aaron, she did not expect them to leave her that battered, bruised and barely alive. That was her job.

Ruby got up from her kitchen table to get a glass of juice as memories of the morning she found Aaron flashed through her mind. Her whole body shivered and she almost dropped her glass as a vivid image of Aaron's face entered her thoughts.

When she found Aaron, she was lying on the bed with bloodstains on the sheet and all over her body. Aaron's face was puffy and bruised, and her eyes had been swollen shut. Her already full lips had doubled from their original size and were a shade of red that was unnatural and too bright for her complexion. Her slightly parted mouth had dry bloodstains that ran from the corners of her lips down to her neck. The way she laid crumpled in the bed initially made Ruby think she was dead until she noticed small, laboured breaths escaping her lips.

All Ruby could do was scream and run. She was surprised at how fearful she really was of death. She remembered having a similar reaction when she had discovered her dead baby sister. Ruby did not blink when confronted by some of the most dangerous men or woman on the streets but facing the Grim Reaper was something she could not handle.

Ruby had already put together a story to tell Aaron about what must have happened but never got the chance to share it. She had tried to visit

Aaron after the nurse informed her that she gained full consciousness. Aaron refused to see Ruby and left very strict instructions with all of the hospital staff on her floor that under no circumstances was Ruby allowed to enter her room.

Her heart began to beat quickly as she started to panic over the whole ordeal. How was she going to get Aaron back into her life after this? Ruby paced back and forth in her small apartment, thinking hard about what she could do. She looked out of her window hoping to gain clarity, but felt insulted by how bright the sun was shining. How dare the sun shine so brilliantly when she felt gloomy and down? She really wished it were raining. That would better match how she was feeling. She closed the blinds that instantly darkened her apartment, and felt a little bit better.

Plopping herself onto her sofa, Ruby pulled her black fur throw over her legs. After a few minutes of plotting, another brilliant plan popped into her head. The only way she could get to Aaron was through the only person she truly loved; Angel. If Ruby had Angel, Aaron would be forced to acknowledge and talk to her. She would be at Ruby's mercy. Now the question became: How could she possibly get Angel?

She was not going to kidnap her or anything. That would be dumb and she was not confident that a plan like that would not send her to jail for life. She had to do it in a way that was legal. Since Angel's birth, Aaron had named Ruby as an emergency contact with her doctors and anywhere else that required that information. Surely, Ruby could use that to her advantage.

"Think Ruby, think," she muttered aloud as her hands flew to the side of her head and entwined in her hair. "There's got to be a way."

Then it came to her. If Angel were taken away from Aaron for whatever reason, she would be given to Ruby. Ruby remembered Esther, a prostitute who had worked the streets for years and disappeared when the Children's Aid Society of Toronto took her three young children away from her. She had a nightly routine during which she would put her kids to bed, go to work and return before they woke up. But one night, the smallest child woke up and cried so loudly that the neighbours called the police. Children's Aid gave the kids to Esther's sister and she had to clean up her life before getting them back. If the same thing happened to Aaron then Angel would be given to Ruby because Aaron had no family. This plan was perfect.

Ruby knew what she had to do. A few phone calls later, she had the number she needed to put her new scheme into action and dialed it without hesitation.

"Children's Aid Society of Toronto. How can I help you?" asked the female voice on the other end.

"I would like to report a situation with a child but need to ensure that I am never identified as the caller."

"Ma'am, I can assure you that you will remain anonymous and any questionable information will be thoroughly investigated. Please hold while I transfer your call," the woman said before putting Ruby on hold.

Ruby was transferred to a caseworker and thirty minutes later hung up the phone, feeling encouraged and hopeful. She gave so much information to the caseworker—both true and false—that Ruby knew she could not be ignored. She painted a picture of Aaron as a mother who was so caught up in a world of crime that she could not provide the necessities required to raise a toddler. She was confident that when they did the investigation and Aaron could not provide any legal way of receiving income, Ruby's story could be confirmed. She also told them about Aaron's rape but created a different story about what happened. According to Ruby's version, Aaron was actually raped by two clients after demanding too much money for her service. After contacting the police who had no answers as to what really happened, Ruby knew Children's Aid would be forced to take action. She had no worries about getting Angel. Aaron would definitely give them her information to care for Angel when they came to take her away. Absolutely brilliant!

Ruby grinned triumphantly. She was given a second chance at her plan and this time, she would not mess it up. Looking around her apartment, she was drawn to a little teddy bear that Angel left behind when she last visited so long ago. A feeling of true longing ripped through her body as she admitted how much she missed that sweet little girl. Walking over to pick up the bear, she realized she needed to make her home kid-friendly so when Children's Aid dropped off Angel, there would be no doubt that her home was suitable. She picked up the Toys "R" Us flyer that was inside the stack of newspapers she was going to drop down the garbage chute and started flipping through it. She was going to have fun preparing for Angel's arrival. She would lavish her with beautiful toys and proper clothes. She laughed out loud thinking about the way Aaron dressed Angel. She was definitely going to replace the goofy character clothing with brands. Ruby would be in full control again and Aaron would have to abide by her rules once and for all. She may even let her baby-sit Angel while she went out and collected her money from her hoes.

Ruby stood up and opened the blinds. This time she welcomed the shining sun with an ear-to-ear smile. She hummed a familiar song in her head as she was filled from head-to-toe with a burst of happiness and a sense of victory.

"Oh Mr. Sun, Sun, Mr. Golden Sun, please shine down on me!"

Yes, Mr. Sun was definitely welcome now.

Twenty One † Aaron

My baby is home now and everything is going to be okay. After everything that happened to me recently, my strength is deeply embedded in my little girl. She is the only hope I have now and I vow to guard her with my life.

I still cannot believe what Ruby did to me. There is no doubt in my mind that she was the mastermind behind my rape and I am almost certain one of the men who raped me mentioned my *friend* but I was in such shock that I cannot be completely sure. I still get angry with myself for falling for her lies and trickery, and believing that she was happy for me. I knew Ruby better than anyone else and should have sensed she was being phony.

Since I met Ruby, I always felt a little overwhelmed by her protection and need to constantly have my attention. She was jealous and wanted me to depend on her for everything. Although she was worse than any man I had ever been with, when we first met and I was still vulnerable to the streets, her need to take care of me was comforting. With Ruby, I felt that old confidence I once had in my father. It did not take me long to understand her street credibility and to feel strength from it. Nobody could even look at me sideways without Ruby getting up in his or her face. I was protected. I was safe.

When I started expressing a need for my own place, Ruby hesitantly hooked me up with one of the hottest apartments on the block. She never told me how she was able to get it, but she did. I was then taught how to market my body for money so I could pay my bills. She never even made me pay dues like all the other girls and I got to keep every cent of the money I earned. My need for independence, however, continued to grow and I started making my own appointments with clients. I also no longer invited her along to act as a bodyguard outside of the places I turned tricks. After about a year of prostitution, I was confident in my abilities and did not need her all up in my business at all. Everyone knew I was her right hand and that alone was protection enough. She definitely was not happy with me. We argued a lot and sometimes I felt like she was going to hurt me but Ruby never beat me up or slapped me around the way she did the other girls. She treated me like her little sister and I knew how she felt. I can admit that sometimes, I took extreme advantage of her love and used her for my own selfish purposes.

Losing me must have been a low point in her life or a blow to her ego and she wanted to teach me a lesson.

"Bitch!" I say, as images of that night flash through my head and a tear trickles down my face.

We were having such a good time and I actually loved Ruby more than ever when she gave me support and encouragement about my new life. To wake up to two thugs standing over me, smelling like liquor, urine and sweat, is something I will never forget.

The only thing that puzzles me is why she was trying so hard to visit me at the hospital afterward. It could not have been out of concern since she set up the whole thing. It had to be to laugh in my face. I definitely did not give her the satisfaction. I hope with all my might that something awful happens to her. She deserves a slow and painful death for what she did to me.

All my dreams and plans vanished, and have been replaced with emptiness. If anything, Ruby showed me that I was living a lie. Thoughts of Brandon invade my mind along with torrents of grief, and I know there is no way I can go back to him. I grieve him as though he has died and feel an extreme pain from my loss—physically and emotionally. The memory of Brandon looking at me with sympathy in his eyes is too much to bear. It would not be long before he realized that I was just a dirty girl playing a role. That sympathy would be replaced by resentment, hatred and disgust, and I was not going to wait around for it to happen.

Nothing about me is the same, nothing! Even my *million-dollar vagina* is now worthless. I had to receive ten stitches to repair the damage those thugs inflicted. I did not even need stitches when I gave birth to Angel. Adding to my humiliation were the tests they ran to make sure I did not have any sexually transmitted diseases or was pregnant. There were many used condoms in the room but they did not want to leave anything to chance.

Then there is my face. I now have a scar that runs from the side of my temple to my ear. It is pretty much covered when I wear my hair down but ponytails or up 'dos will no longer be an option in public. I have no idea when and how I got cut because I do not remember the details of the night but I am pretty sure I had to sustain a good thrashing to get it. How ironic; both Brandon and I now have scars.

My body pretty much has recovered but I have a bit of trouble remembering small things. I find that sometimes I will get up to get something and by the time I make it to my destination, I cannot remember what I needed. My doctor says I might recover from this. He believes it is a form of shock or memory loss from my suffering. I personally think it is from the bashing I got but I am not a doctor. I hope that I recover entirely so I can move on.

The worst outcome is my lack of confidence and new sense of fear. I no longer feel sexy or attractive and the thought of men makes me shiver. I never want a man to touch me again—ever! How can I marry someone or even be with someone for that manner? What a great conversation that would be:

"Hey, I'll marry you. But just so you know, you can never make love to me, or kiss or hug me!"

I do not know how I survived all these years drama-free with all the men I serviced. Anything could have happened to me but never did. How ironic that I was harmed after I decided to retire. Actually; it makes total sense. Ruby was the one who protected me over the years and she was the same person who harmed me. Without her protection, I was defenseless.

What I find really weird is the way Brandon had tried to stop me from meeting with Ruby. How on earth did he sense the danger to which I was so clueless? It makes no sense. He tried so many times to visit me at the hospital and I turned him away. It was the hardest thing to do but it was necessary. There were a few times I almost broke down and contacted him, but what would I say? He was saving himself for me for our wedding night, and my body was ravished and abused. I am soiled and nothing can change that.

Walking away from Brandon and that joke of an engagement is the best decision I could ever make. I just have to wait for my heart to agree with my mind and let him go. I know I will get over him; it just takes time. I mean, I got over my family, right? Even as these thoughts enter my head, I know they are wrong. Getting over my family was easier because they had inflicted so many calamities in my life that walking away was liberating and I never looked back.

Brandon was different. He showered me with love and affection. He made my life count. He treated me like a queen and made me actually believe I was one. He gave me a purpose aside from being a mom. No, it will not be easy to get over him but I have to. I have no choice. I love him enough to let him go. He deserves better. He deserves a regular woman who has a good past that will compliment his lifestyle. He deserves a successful professional whom he could show off to the world. I never was and never could be that woman.

A heavy knock at the door jolts me out of my thoughts. It takes me a minute to make sense of my whereabouts and I feel grateful for the interruption.

"Who is it?" I call out cautiously as I walk towards the door.

I no longer open my door without first confirming who it is.

"Aaron Hope, it's the police. Please open the door!" a deep voice replies.

I am a bit surprised that they did not call me first since I have been speaking a lot with Detective Brown, who keeps me updated in any new findings of my case. They must have some important news to make a house call. I open the door and am surprised to see two unfamiliar police officers and a plain-clothed woman.

"Can I help you?" I ask, a bit confused.

The woman is the first to speak.

"Miss Hope, I am Mrs. Donovan and I work for the Children's Aid Society of Toronto. I am the caseworker assigned to your family. Due to recent concerns brought to our attention, we have no choice but to remove," she looks down at her notepad to get the correct name, "Angel Hope from your care until a further investigation has taken place."

"What?" I say, a little dumbfounded and pissed off at the same time. "Take who? You are not taking my baby. Is this some kind of joke?" I step with my shoulders squared to Mrs. Donovan so we are nose-to-nose.

What is going on? As I stare down the caseworker, the policewoman steps forward, giving me a stern look. It dawns on me that they are not are here about my case. This is something very different but I am still confused about what is happening.

Mrs. Donovan raises her hand to the officer as if signaling that everything is under control.

"Miss Hope..." she begins.

"Aaron!" I interrupt.

"Okay, Aaron, please understand that I am not here to make your life miserable. I am here to help. Some serious allegations have been made against you, which concern your daughter and her safety. Until the matter is cleared, she must be removed from your home." She hands me a card with her name, number and address. "If everything turns out okay, she will be returned to your home as soon as possible. I know this is difficult, but can you please bring her to me with some of her favourite toys and a few articles of clothing?"

I cannot believe the audacity of this woman. She has the nerve to march up into my home and think I am just going to hand my child over to her. She has another thing coming.

"Are you bullshitting me? You think I am going to bring you my daughter and her things, and give her to you like that? What concerns? My rape? You are trying to punish me for being raped by taking away my daughter?" Frantic tears start streaming down my face as my voice, filled with hatred, anger and desperation raises another notch, "What kind of justice is that?"

The male officer steps to me this time and speaks without an ounce of compassion in his voice.

"Miss Hope, we can either do this the easy way or the hard way. If I were you, I would choose the easy way, for the benefit of you and your daughter."

Mrs. Donovan looks me right in my eyes and, even though she is my archenemy right now, I can feel her empathy. In this instant I can see that this part of her job is not easy nor is it something she wants to do. I glance at the two police officers, who look ready to do whatever is necessary, and then turn my head towards the room where my sweet Angel is sleeping.

My story is not going to have a happy ending. They are leaving with Angel, whether I fight them or not. A loud sob escapes my lips.

"Aaron," Mrs. Donovan says in a gentle tone, "like I said, I need to do this until our investigation is finalized. This has nothing to do with your recent rape. I am sorry that happened to you. We are following up on some information that was reported to our office. Due to the serious nature of the information, we have orders to immediately remove Angel from your care. I will do everything I can to have her returned to you as soon as possible, but I need you to cooperate. Trust me, cooperation works in your favour."

She is actually pleading with me with her eyes. I am not sure what it is but I know I can trust her and she does not want the situation to escalate to uncontrollable proportions.

Feeling defeated, I walk into my room where Angel is still sleeping in the middle of my bed with pillows around her to keep her safe. Mrs. Donovan follows but keeps a respectful distance between us. I figure she had to supervise me to ensure I do not try to do something crazy out of desperation. I stand over Angel and watch her sleep for a minute and then like a robot, I grab her baby bag and carefully place inside a few outfits, diapers, wipes and other necessities. I pick up some of her toys and place them into the bag last but hold onto her favourite Dora doll and walk over to Mrs. Donovan.

"Dora is her most-loved toy right now. Please make sure she always has her near," I whisper with as much courage as I can gather.

Mrs. Donovan nods, letting me know she understands. I turn and carefully lift my sleeping Angel off the bed. I do not have the heart to wake her, so I hold her tenderly to my chest and softly kiss the untamed curls at the top of her head. I walk back over to Mrs. Donovan and place Angel into her arms, hoping she does not wake up. I cannot bear to have her witness me handing her over to a bunch of strangers like she is valueless.

"Thank you, Aaron," says Mrs. Donovan with a reassuring smile. "Remember, I am here to help and will be in touch with you as soon as possible. Feel free to contact me at the number on the card."

I turn my back to her. Her voice was making me angry. How could she be doing such a terrible thing and yet make me feel drawn to her at the same time?

"Please go now," I whimper.

After a few seconds of complete silence, I hear Mrs. Donovan turn and leave. I wait until I hear the front door close before I walk out of the bedroom. I somehow manage to walk over to the front door and lock it before I collapse to the floor in a heap of failure. My life is now over.

I sit in shock on my floor with my back against the front door and clutch my knees to my chest and bawl. I cry until I feel there were no more tears and even then, I manage to squeeze out more.

I do not know how long I sit there as the events that just took place overtake me like a flash of lightening but when I look up, my apartment is cloaked in darkness.

What could I have done to deserve this? What did my dear Angel do to deserve this? Who called? Was it Brandon, Ruby or someone else? Who hates me this much? Tears flow down my cheeks as my eyes burn from the salt in my tears. Although I eventually stumble to my bed, it is hours before I fall asleep. When I do, my dreams are filled with scenes of my traumatic past.

That morning when I was leaving for school, something was not right. Daddy seemed to be lost in another world and was definitely not himself. I was thirteen and was used to the same morning routine since I started kindergarten. Normally, I came downstairs and was instantly wrapped in daddy's arms. After a few hugs and kisses, I would sit at the table while daddy prepared breakfast for me. No matter what I requested, he made it. I always stared with adoration at my daddy as he prepared my meals because I knew he loved me. None of my friends' fathers made breakfast for them. Most of them made breakfast for themselves. This was just one of the ways daddy made me feel special. There were so many other things but starting my morning like this kept me on cloud nine throughout the day. I knew I was his princess and he was my king.

No matter how often we moved, it didn't take long before everyone in the neighbourhood knew my daddy. He was good looking and everything about him was flashy—watches, car, home, clothes, wife and child included. My mother always looked beautiful and I always had on the latest gear. I never knew what kind of work he did. The one time I actually asked, he told me to never ask him again. In my heart, I knew that whatever he did, he was good at it and he was respected.

The jealous girls in my neighbourhood sometimes made up stories about what my daddy did. According to them, he was a drug dealer, a hit man or a con artist but I knew better than that. I believed that my daddy worked for the C.I.A or something similar and that was why he did not want me to know. They could think what they wanted. I really did not care.

While my daddy showered me with attention, my mom did not have time for me. She was too selfish. She spent her days getting her hair and nails done or shopping, and her nights partying. She even told me not to call her mom because she felt too young to have a child. Instead, I called her by her first name. She did not matter to me though, because my daddy showed me enough love to compensate for her lack of interest.

That particular morning, daddy did not hug or kiss me and he did not make me breakfast. He kept pacing back and forth in the kitchen, and checked his phone every few minutes. I knew better than to bother him. The tension in the room was obvious. I grabbed a bowl of cereal for breakfast and was surprised that daddy did not object. I do not even think he was aware of my presence until I headed for the door and told him goodbye.

"Listen, I want you to go home with your friend Jackie today and stay there until I come and get you," he said in a tone he had never used towards me. "Under no circumstances do you go anywhere. Do not talk to anyone and go straight to her house. Do you understand?" I nodded my understanding and headed for the door.

Jackie did not come to school that day but I still went to her house after school. I figured no one was home because there were no cars on the driveway but still knocked and rang her bell for close to an hour before I left. I did not know what to do or where to go, so I headed in the direction of my house. On the way there, I stopped and used the payphone at the local convenience store to ask my daddy what he wanted me to do. He did not answer the house phone or his cell phone so I decided to go home. I had nowhere else to go and besides that, my daddy had given me strict instructions not to go anywhere else.

When I arrived, I was surprised to see daddy's car on the driveway since he had not answered the phone. Disregarding all the instructions he gave me earlier, I burst through the doors, calling out to him.

"Hi, daddy! I'm home."

There was no answer and I followed the hallway down to the living room but froze when I saw my mom and dad seated in chairs with four men standing around the room. My mom was crying and daddy's face was swollen. He met my eyes with both worry and anger. I could tell he was upset that I did not listen to him but I had no time to explain before I was roughly grabbed by one of the men, who held my arms behind my back.

"Well, well, well what have we here?" the man said in a creepy way. "Look who finally decided to join us."

He let go of one of my arms to run his fingers along my face. Chills ran up and down my spine.

"Leave her alone. She's just a kid," my daddy begged the stranger, who only seemed to take pleasure in hearing him sound desperate. "I'll do whatever you want. I'll get you your money, just let her go!" he screamed.

Immediately, another man took his gun and slapped my daddy across the face with it. I screamed loudly and desperately tried to pull away to help my daddy, who was bleeding so much. Looking at my mom, I realized that she had been roughed up as well. I did not know what was happening but I knew I had to help.

The man holding me pushed me towards one of the other strangers who grabbed me around the waist. He walked up to my daddy and bent down so he could be eye level with him.

"Too late," he said. "I gave you enough time. It's time to teach you who you're messing with. I don't play with my money."

He turned and nodded to the guy holding me, who pushed me on the sofa and started pulling off my pants.

"Daddy!" I screamed helplessly as I kicked and fought, knowing it was pointless.

My daddy could not help me. No one could. My mom's cries were reduced to a whimper after a hard slap and I turned to look at my daddy. His head was down and he was shaking.

I was raped, right in front of my mom and daddy. Even though I had a boyfriend, we never went all the way and I was a virgin. The men cheered, hooted and yelled insults at my daddy. When the man finished violating me, he kissed me on the cheek and whispered in my ear that I could thank my daddy for what happened.

After they all left, I sat on the sofa, crying and afraid to move. All I wanted was my daddy to comfort me, hold me and tell me everything would be all right. Instead, he screamed at me that I did not listen. He yelled insults at my mother and me before storming out. Without extending any words of comfort to me, my mom went upstairs into her room and did not come out. I was left to lick my own wounds. No one called the police or even took me to see a doctor. I was told to keep my mouth shut and a few days later, we moved.

Nothing was the same after that. Daddy withdrew completely and never looked at me the same way. Now when his eyes met mine, they were full of hatred. I felt like he blamed me for everything, and I knew explaining why I disobeyed him and came home would not change anything. Mom barely ever spoke a word to me and I became the victim of verbal abuse from my daddy. Everything I did was wrong. I knew this was his way of dealing with what happened and having to witness my rape, but what was mine? How was I supposed to heal?

One day, I came home from school to find my daddy sitting at the table with an empty bottle of rum in front of him. I had never seen him look so weak and pathetic. His clothes were crumpled and his face was unshaven. He looked up when I entered the room.

"She left me. That bitch up and left me!" he slurred then started to laugh hysterically. "After all I did for her, she up and left me, and told me I could keep the kid."

I figured he was talking about my mom and was not surprised to hear any of this. She never really loved my daddy, only the lifestyle he provided, and I was always just a nuisance to her. After the world of luxury and power was taken away, she had no reason to stay. She definitely did not love me.

Then my daddy looked up, and smiled at me with love and warmth. For a minute, I felt that familiar feeling that I had been deprived of for so long. He motioned me over with a wave of his arm and then pulled me onto his lap. He hugged me tightly, and I felt so safe and secure in his arms. My daddy lifted my face to his and started kissing me in a way I knew was wrong.

"What are you doing?" I said as I pulled my face away from his.

He grinned at me, as his breathing became heavy and thick. The stench of alcohol on his breath filled my nostrils.

"Now that your mom is gone, I'm going to teach you the proper way a woman should love a man," he said as he started rubbing my thighs. "I won't do it the way that man did. I am going to teach you how to enjoy it."

I jumped off his lap and backed up, creating a good distance between us.

"Daddy, what are you doing? This is wrong!" I screamed.

He looked at me with hatred and lust spilling from his eyes. I knew his intentions and I refused to let it happen. I would die first. I bolted from the kitchen, grabbed my emergency backpack, which was hidden in the front closet, and bolted through the door. I ran and ran, and never turned back.

I wake up from dreams of my childhood and realize that I am lying on my bed in my street clothes. The events of what took place earlier flood my mind and I am overcome by a heaviness that I cannot bear. I do not know why, but I call out to the God I heard about many times in my life.

"God, what have I ever done to you to deserve this awful life you handed me? First, you took my daddy away then Brandon and now my baby! Why are you doing this? What did I do to you?" I cry out in between sobs. "If you exist, fix this. Please fix my life. Change it because I can't take anymore! Sorry for whatever I did that was so wrong but please, I need your help!"

I cry and cry until I am truly empty. I need to be held, rocked and reassured by someone that everything was going to be okay. I want to call Brandon but I am too ashamed. Ruby is definitely off limits and I cannot call Carm. She is too young to be of any comfort. When I realize that I have no one to turn to, I make a very important decision. I do not want this life anymore. I refuse to live this life. I need it all to end. It is too much. Forget God; He cannot not help me. Nobody can.

With renewed strength, I get up, go to my bathroom and find the pain medication that was prescribed to me when I got my wisdom teeth removed. I never used it because I did not like to take any form of medication. None of my prior beliefs matter anymore.

Going back into the bedroom and seeing Angel's empty crib and deserted Dora toys overpowers me. I feel nothing but sorrow as I stare at reminders of my baby. I grab the first teddy bear Angel had received at the hospital when she was born, and sit on my bed embracing it. I open the bottle of pills and put one in my mouth then decide to call on God one more time with a request.

"God, if you can hear me, all I want you to do for me is take care of my baby girl. Don't let her suffer the way I did and give her a better life than I had. Trust me; I suffered enough in this life for the both of us. Please let her know her mommy loved her." I whisper.

Slowly, I put pill after pill in my mouth. I know what is happening but it feels like a dream. No one will miss me, and they will probably find me only when my body starts to stink. This makes me laugh because I am very particular about my hygiene and the thought of me stinking up the place is amusing. Oh, what a comfort humor is to me as I face death.

As I go to put another pill in my mouth, I realize that I cannot not move. It feels like warm arms have been wrapped around me and my arms are too heavy to lift. Odd, I think, it must be the effects of the pills kicking in. Who knew that dying could feel so peaceful? I find comfort in the feeling and give up on trying to swallow the rest of the pills. I want to cry but cannot, nor can I open my eyes. I start to feel like I am floating on a fluffy cloud.

The last moments of my life should have been met with tears and not peace. I feel the arms of my mother, my daddy, Ruby, Brandon and Angel entwined as one, embracing me like a child. My mind drifts back to the good days of my youth then to the birth of Angel and then to wonderful moments with Brandon. I am thankful that the last memories of my life are only filled with happiness. I guess this is what it feels like to have your life flash before your eyes. I also smile knowing that Angel will be taken care of. She will have me as her guardian angel and I will always protect her.

"I will never forsake you or leave you," the voice whispers to me.

At its sound, I feel comfort and security, and I am filled with an overwhelming feeling of contentment. With a smile, I welcome death as the new chapter of my existence.

PART ✝ TWO

Trust in the Lord with all your heart and lean not on your own understandings; in all your ways submit to him, and he will make your paths straight.

Twenty Two † Brandon

Brandon decided that Karl might be his only likelihood for comfort. Karl had helped him through the gripping emotional pain when he learned about his ex-wife's infidelity and filed for divorced. He hoped Karl would be supportive again. Although Brandon deemed Karl a *Bible thumper*, he always had a way of comforting Brandon with a sense of peace that seemed to ooze from his pores. He also had an air of wisdom that made Brandon feel like Karl knew something he did not. He dealt with all of his problems differently and almost always spoke positively about any situation. Brandon often felt annoyed by Karl but right now, he craved his knowledge.

After arranging to meet up at a Starbucks in the suburb of Mississauga, it was not long before Karl arrived. This was their meet-up spot when they wanted to avoid the hustle and bustle of the downtown core.

Karl waved at Brandon and went directly to the counter to order his favourite latte. He then joined Brandon, who was already sipping his tall order of black coffee. He did not want a fluffy drink today. He required the strong stuff. After exchanging their infamous handshake, Karl sat down. Brandon gave him a quick once-over and then went straight into his story. He needed to get everything out before he changed his mind.

"Karl, I don't know what to do. I don't know how to get over her. I don't even know if I want to get over her..."

As Brandon continued his story, he told Karl everything from how he met Aaron and how they built their relationship to how she called off their wedding. He left out no details.

"I've been paying her for sex for over a year Karl waiting for the moment when I could win her over..."

He waited for Karl to react, but his friend sat quietly, acting as though Brandon was not sharing the most shocking news. Brandon was beginning to wonder if he was listening, but Karl nodded and smiled, encouraging him to continue.

"I asked her not to go, I begged her but she didn't listen. I don't know why or how but I knew something was wrong with the girl's night. Dammit, I shouldn't have allowed her to go Karl. I should have listened to my gut and now, I feel like I've lost her forever..."

When Brandon finished, he put his head in his hands and waited for Karl to speak. When he heard nothing, he slowly lifted his head up to see if Karl was still there. Karl just looked at him and smiled.

"Umm, aren't you going to say anything?" asked Brandon, confused by Karl's lack of reaction.

"Sometimes, the best thing to say is nothing at all," Karl replied and took another sip of his latte.

He pulled out his BlackBerry and busied himself with emails. Brandon was ticked. He did not pour out his soul to Karl to get no feedback. Karl was being a selfish jerk. He really needed him to speak right now. Whether Karl's reaction was good or bad, he needed to hear something.

"Aw, hell naw," Brandon said. "When I don't want you to say nothing, you speak. But now that I desperately need to hear your opinion, you say nothing. You have nothing to say about me falling in love with a prostitute?" He did not care if anyone overheard him.

Karl put down his BlackBerry, cleared his throat, sat up and looked Brandon straight in the eye.

"First of all, anything I have to say will not change your situation because it will only be my opinion. Second, she is still a woman, whether she is or was a prostitute. When you are speaking to me, address her respectfully. No matter what, we are all children of God and you should address her as one. If you want my opinion so badly, that's the first thing you need to change."

Brandon could not believe that Karl was only focusing on a title and not the meat and potatoes of the story.

"I'm only telling you what she did as a profession to explain the story to you. I never, ever threw that in her face. It was never an issue to me; don't get it twisted. Karl, I want your opinion, whether it will change the situation or not," Brandon said, still not understanding why Karl was choosing to be so difficult.

Karl opened his mouth to say something but quickly closed it. He closed his eyes for a split second and appeared to be reviewing what he was about to say. Brandon always admired Karl's strength. He seemed to have control over his thoughts and his words, and never spoke without thinking.

"Since you want my opinion, Brandon, here it is. Seek God about your situation because only He holds the answer you need. If she is meant to be with you, she will be. It does not matter if she is a prostitute, doctor or a lawyer. If you love her with your entire heart and soul, and truly know she is the one for you, ask God for guidance."

Karl sat back and he seemed to relax. He smiled warmly at Brandon.

"Come to church with me on Sunday. It will do you a tremendous amount of good."

Brandon could not believe what he was hearing and wanted to reach across the table to choke Karl. Of all the times he could have gone into his *Bible thumping* routine, he chose now. Really? What a coward! He did not want to answer the question directly and give his true opinion so he danced around it with tales of God and church. Was he for real?

"Thanks for absolutely nothing, Karl. Thanks for being *such* a good friend," Brandon blurted out in a childish, sarcastic manner.

Without another word, he rose from the table and stormed out of the Starbucks. He was seething. How dare Karl tell him bullshit at a time like this? There was a time and place for everything. Talking about his dilemma to some unseen God was not going to help him. Sure, Brandon was familiar with God. He was raised Catholic and as a boy, had gone to church. But he did not think going to church and confessing his sins behind a velvet curtain would make a difference in his life. His situation needed real, tangible help.

As he was about to back his car out of the parking spot, Karl came up and tapped on his window. Brandon lowered it but did not turn to face Karl.

"I know you're mad because I didn't fix your problem but if you change your mind, I'll be here on Sunday. I am an usher during the morning service but I attend the eleven thirty service. I am always close to the front of the church if you want to find me. All the information you need is on here," he said as he handed Brandon a church program and walked away. Talk about putting salt on a fresh wound.

Brandon sped so quickly out of the parking lot that he would not have been surprised if he smelled burnt rubber. Leave it to Karl to make light of how angry Brandon was with him. Brandon should have known better than to call him. There was no way on earth he was going to church. God didn't help Brandon before, so why would he help him now? When he had prayed for Aaron and she had fallen in love with him, for a minute, he thought God had his back. Then it all fell apart. Forget it! There had to be someone else who could help him. Karl was a complete write-off!

Twenty Three † Aaron

I cannot explain why I am still alive or why I feel at peace, but I do. It has been exactly two weeks to the day that Angel was taken away from me, and I have never felt better. I know this does not sound right, but it is the truth. Period.

I have tried so hard to remember the dream I had when I attempted to take my life but cannot seem to. All I can remember is feeling harmony and a love that I never felt before. Without confirmation, I know it was God. Somehow, He heard my cries and came through.

I woke up the next day with a headache like you would not believe but that is the point: I woke up! I am still alive and breathing. I was given a second chance at life. How stupid could I have been to try to take my life knowing how much Angel needs me? It was an extremely selfish thing to do and I am glad I was unsuccessful. After waking up, I counted the pills that were missing from the bottle and was dumbfounded at what I discovered. According to my count, only four pills were missing but I swear I took more than that. Let me reiterate: I am one hundred percent positive that I swallowed more than four pills. Unbelievable!

I also remember the voice telling me it would never leave me. I finally figured out to whom the voice belongs and now that I want it to speak to me, I hear nothing. The voice has now been replaced with a new lease on life. I choose life.

Angel has been placed in a temporary home, which I was assured is safe and full of love. I have to take parenting classes and do drug tests. Whoever called Children's Aid said that I worked the streets, frequently left my baby home alone and had clients in my bed every night. You and I both know that two of those statements are false. It is obvious the person wanted to bury me. The accuser also said that the rape happened while I was with clients and that is why I am not cooperating fully with the police by disclosing the names of the men who attacked me. The fact that I do not have a job and am not on welfare only made me look more suspicious. Children's Aid wanted to know how I could possibly afford such a great apartment in an affluent neighbourhood with no source of income. I had nothing to tell them. Even if I managed to collect evidence from my recent work decorating homes, it still could not attest for all the prior years.

In the end, I came clean with Mrs. Donovan about my past but let her know what was factual and what was not. Mrs. Donovan was kind and seemed to truly want to reunite me with Angel. She was fair and honest, and told me I had to make many changes in my life before I could get my daughter back.

The weird thing is my supervised visits with Angel and Mrs. Donovan on Wednesdays and Saturdays take place in a church. This might sound like a cliché, but I feel it is a sign. I know I should be upset about not having Angel with me but for some reason, I know I need this. It is a chance for me to totally clean up my life, on my own, and change my future for Angel and me. Mrs. Donovan has promised to help me get into school, and talks to me about my hopes and dreams. I trust her enough to have told her about what happened to me when I was thirteen. I surprised myself when I did because I never told anyone, not even Ruby. When I finished speaking, her eyes were glistening and she looked at me with so much compassion in her eyes. It was the type of look I feel I should have received from my mom. I literally felt the weight of the burden fall off my shoulders and I was truly grateful for her. I feel the empty void caused by my absent mother filling with the attention Mrs. Donovan is giving me and I barely know her. There is something so majestic about her.

She hooked me up with a church counselor who is going to meet with me after today's service. I am nervous about being there on a Sunday. On Wednesdays and Saturdays, there is not much happening but I know that a Sunday will bring loads and loads of people for the service. Nevertheless, I am excited to talk about my life with someone who can help me heal. I need to heal. It is time.

So here I am, standing in front of my closet trying to find something *churchy* to wear. If I remember correctly from movies and television shows, churchwomen are expected to wear hats, frilly dresses and gloves. I do not have a hat or a frilly dress but I do own a pair of black gloves that actually belong to a sexy lingerie ensemble. No one will be any the wiser! I decide on a grey knee-length skirt with a black button-down top that has a hint of frills along the outline of the V-neck, lace pantyhose and my black silk gloves. I finish the look with my black kitten heels and black clutch. That is as close as I can get to a churchy look. I pin my hair up on the left side but let the right side cascade down so it covers my scar. I decide to skip my full face of make-up and opt only for mascara and a touch of pink tinted lip-gloss. I really do not want the church to burn down when I enter and need desperately to blend in.

Thirty minutes later, I am on my way. I contemplate parking a few blocks away so I am not seen arriving in my flashy Benz because everyone knows church people drive old Fords and Pontiacs. I arrive a few minutes early and decide to just park in the back of the parking lot. Well, am I ever surprised to see all the nice cars? I mean, is that a Jaguar? You have to be kidding me! What kind of church is this? Feeling a little bit better about the situation, I park my car at the closest available parking spot. After gathering my nerves and calming my anxiety, I lock the car and head into the church.

I must say, the exterior of the church does not match the interior. The exterior has that traditional church appearance with the old stone and the stained glass. But the interior...wow. Rich shades of purple, gold and silver complement the oak floors and oak furniture. There is even a red carpet that runs from the entryway of the church to the three sets of double doors ahead. When I come for my visits with Angel on Wednesdays and Saturdays, I go through a side door that leads me to the basement level. I have never entered through the front doors and there is something so mesmerizing about everything. A middle-aged woman, wearing a dark purple, knee-length suit with a colourful scarf, stands at the entry of one of the double doors. She even has on spiked heels and sports the latest haircut. What? Where are the frills?

A quick glance at my watch tells me I am forty minutes early for my appointment and I look around, unsure of what to do. She must feel my apprehension because she smiles.

"Welcome!"

Oh, no. What am I going to do? I do not want to be rude and blow her off but I definitely do not want to go into the service area. I take a deep breath and walk over to her.

"Um, I'm not here for the service. I have a meeting with a counselor and I'm early. Can you please show me where I can wait?"

She smiles at me with a knowing glance and hands me a program.

"Sweetheart, God brought you this far. All you need to do is go through the doors. Besides," she adds with a bit of mischief in her voice, "you have to go through the main area to get to the offices."

I look at her with fear stricken eyes. I absolutely cannot not go in. What if all the church people see through me? What was I thinking coming here? This has to be some kind of joke. But I realize I have no choice so I mumble a thank-you, take a deep breath, muster all the courage I can and walk in. What did she mean by God brought me this far? What did He want with me? I look around at the body of people gathered for the service and wonder what we could possibly have in common. At first glance, I can tell that none of them have ever experienced any hardships—much less the shameful events that have taken place in my life. The peace I felt earlier evaporates and is replaced with resentment.

Look at them, crying and clapping and dancing as if they are on something. Oh yeah, I have done all these things at one time in my life or another, but not at the same time. I would never feel comfortable here. This is too much and it is bullshit! What a bunch of hypocrites. Instead of wasting their time here, why are they not out there helping those in need?

A gentleman in a full purple pantsuit steps forward and beckons me to follow him. He must be crazy. I shake my head and step back until I am in the corner. If I have to stay, I will not be sitting amongst them. Then it happens. She speaks and, at once, everyone sits down. There is something powerful in her voice that commands not only their attention but also mine. She looks like an angel and her smile lights up the room. I wonder who she is and why the pastor isn't up there. Then she says the words that I will never forget:

"Even a prostitute is God's creation and Jesus Christ died so she could be welcomed as his child. The blood of Jesus makes even a prostitute sinless. All she has to do is ask Him to come into her heart."

She goes on to preach about someone named Mary Magdalene or Marmalade or something but I cannot focus. My head started to spin at the mention of the prostitute. Why had she said that at the exact moment I walked into the room? How could I be God's creation and sinless because of someone else's blood? I am overcome with a dizziness that I cannot control. She has me mesmerized. Am I the only one in the room who feels this way? Why is it that everything she says lines up with events in my life?

A part of me feels set up. The counselor must have known I would have to go through the auditorium to get to the office and told this woman what to say because there is no way this is coincidence. The wiser part of me knows better as she talks about pain and hardships in life, and God being there for us through everything. People are openly crying and I have to fight back tears. I feel as though I am going to faint and wish I had not refused a seat.

"God wants you to bring Him all your problems, your pain and your insecurities, and leave them at the altar. He wants to take all your burdens away and give you a fresh start on life—a brand new life in Him. He wants you to take His hand and welcome Him into your heart. Won't you welcome Him into your heart today? If you do not know Jesus like you should know Him, I ask you to come to the altar and let us pray for you. Won't you come and meet with Him today?"

I do not know when, why or how it happened but I am walking towards the front of the church. I cannot help myself. It must have been the faint feeling I had or the magic that seemed to be in the air but a few seconds later, I am at the altar with other people and I am weeping. In front of this packed church, I am crying my eyes out. My nose is running and I am sure my mascara is too but I do not care. I want what she talked about. I feel a hand on my back encouraging me to move forward to one of the women assigned to pray for people. The woman who is speaking on stage encourages everyone at the front to come even closer because God's arms are wide open. I make eye contact with her for a brief moment and her smile encourages me to move forward. I want to get closer to this woman so I kind of sidestep the lady waiting to pray for me and go directly to the edge of the stage. I need to be close to her. I look up at her and she reaches her hand to me with a meaningful look. She speaks directly to me, mic and all, but I do not care. I no longer feel any shame.

"My daughter," she says, "do you know Jesus Christ as your personal Lord and Saviour?"

I slowly shake my head as I receive her hand.

"Would you like to receive Him as your personal Lord and Saviour today?"

I nod my head as I squeeze her hand.

She says a few words then asks me to repeat that I repent of my sins and invite Jesus Christ into my heart as my lord and saviour. After I declare this, I feel overcome with the most awesome feeling. It is not an electric type of feeling but rather one of liberty. I feel myself stagger backwards slightly and I am shocked when I fall into somebody's arms. The person hugs and holds me as I weep. Moments later, I look up and realize it is the woman who was supposed to pray for me. She whispers in my ear.

"God welcomes you into His family and Kingdom. You are washed clean and free of your past. He has given you His greatest gift, which is a brand new life in Him. We love you and welcome you."

I turn and embrace her for a very, very long time while letting the beautiful song the choir is singing fill me from head to toe. All I know is that I have been given a new life and from now on, everything was going to be okay.

Twenty Four † Ruby

"Look here, if I don't get my money by Friday—all of it—you are going to be one sorry little chick!" Ruby said as she held one of her hookers by the neck and squeezed until the girl started to choke.

Just to make her point clear, she slapped the girl so hard in the back of the head that she stumbled to the ground.

"Friday!" She repeated as she purposely stepped over the weeping girl and walked out of the shoddy bar.

The night air was a little brisk but Ruby hardly noticed. This whole situation with Aaron had her slipping and her girls were trying to take advantage of it.

The girl she roughed up was called Glimmer on the streets, and Ruby had found out she was booking clients on the side and pocketing all the money. That is not how it worked and she would be damned if she let another little bitch get away with anything else. She learned her lesson with Aaron. Ruby patrolled one of the streets in Toronto most famous for prostitution, making sure all her girls knew she was back in full force. If she kept slipping the way she had been lately, they would finally get some common sense and maybe bond together, and leave her. She worked hard to build her reputation and she was not going to lose it all for Mickey Mouse shit.

As she walked the streets checking to see that the girls were at their stations, she wondered why she had not yet been contacted about taking care of Angel. It had been quite some time since she placed the call to Children's Aid and when she tried to follow up on her report, they informed her that whatever actions, if any, were confidential. She was pissed off and told the caseworker as much but was informed that although the organization was thankful for her concern, it was not obligated to follow up with her. What was it going to take to make things work? Ruby was getting fed up and irate with everything.

She had blocked her number and called Aaron the other day but her phone was out of service. She knew Aaron changed her number so Ruby could not contact her. After discovering Aaron's number was no longer in service, she almost went to her apartment but changed her mind at the last minute. She knew Aaron would be upset about losing Angel and did not want her to call the police. Her gut instinct told her to wait a while before attempting to make any contact. Ruby needed Aaron's friendship more than anyone would ever know. She was lonely, depressed and fragile. Yeah, she put on a tough face for the girls on the street but her inside did not match the outside. All this stress had her dropping weight like a crack head. Ruby was always thick and prided herself on looking butch, but her weight loss made her more curvy and girly looking. It was like she was losing who she was altogether.

To make matters even worse, two day ago, she had to put down her cat—the one she rescued when she had met Aaron. The cat was old and crapping all over the apartment. A visit to the vet confirmed she was dying and the best thing to do was to put her down. She loved that cat so much and could not bear to see her suffer the way she did. She made an appointment with the vet, said a quick good-bye and just left her there. She did not know if she would survive losing anything else in her life.

Having Angel would have been the answer to all her problems right now. Angel would fill her empty home and heart with giggles and much needed warmth. Angel would also lead Aaron back into her life. But it looked like another one of her brilliant plans had failed. She did not have any more good ideas up her sleeve.

After Ruby was certain all her girls were doing their jobs, she decided it was okay to head home. There was nothing else she needed to do and nobody to hang out with. She was just about to hail a cab when a familiar but unwelcome voice called out.

"Ruby! Hey, Ruby!"

Ruby rolled her eyes to make it clear that she was not interested.

"What the heck do you want, Joe? What's it going to take for you to leave me alone?" she asked.

Joe smiled at Ruby as though this question was the perfect lead in to what he wanted to say.

"Well, you could let me take you out on one date. If you give me one date, I will never bug you again—ever," he replied with a sheepish grin.

Ruby was about to burst Joe's world with a big "hell-to-the-no" but something about him was different tonight. She looked him up and down, and realized that Joe actually looked...decent. It did not take her long to figure out what it was. Joe had cut his shoulder length curly hair to the nape of his neck, and a fresh new outfit that consisted of jeans, a tee and a leather jacket replaced his usual dress pants and goofy bow tie. It looked like Joe had gotten some advice because he suddenly seemed to know how important image was to Ruby. But even with the attire and cut, she knew he was the same old goofy Joe.

"What's up with the new look, Joe? Are you trying to impress someone?" she asked with a grin on her face as she realized that right now Joe could be a pleasant and humorous diversion.

"You bet!" Joe said without hesitation. "You!" he smiled.

Until a few months ago, Ruby had been unaware of how much Joe really liked her. Then, on a whim, he asked her to be his wife right in front of all the thugs on the street. Ruby blew him off and left him on his knees on the sidewalk.

"So, let me get this straight. You thought a haircut and new clothes would make me agree to go on a date with you?" she asked with absolutely no interest in her voice.

"Well, not exactly," he said. "But I was hoping that I was on the right track. I'm willing to change anything for one date with you, Ruby."

Ruby hesitated for a minute then swore inwardly as it hit her that loneliness was the deciding factor in her answer. She rolled her eyes and took a deep breath.

"Okay, Joe, you win. You went through a lot of trouble to impress me so I'm willing to go on one date with you but," she paused for emphasis, "you better not try to take me to no cheesy restaurant or lovey-dovey movie. I don't play that. Understand?"

"Understand!" Joe replied a bit too eagerly.

Ruby wondered what she was getting herself into. She suddenly felt a weird attraction to Joe and realized she had never noticed how beautiful his eyes were. The green in his eyes almost glowed against his dark olive complexion. His black hair now suited him since it was cut. He had a strong jaw line, which was balanced by a very nice set of teeth. He was skinny, a bit too skinny, but the new clothing complimented his physique and made him look a little less wimpy. She wondered if Joe was a good kisser or if he had ever kissed a girl.

"So, what, you gonna stand there looking at me all night or are you going to ask for my number?" she asked trying to regain control over the situation. She was not herself and did not know if she liked this new feeling. Joe took her number and promised to call her the next day with a time and place for their date. She let him know it had to be somewhere far from downtown. She could not risk being seen with him by anyone she knew on the streets. She also made him promise not to say anything to the local thugs. Joe waited with her until she flagged a cab. She was not inside the cab for more than two minutes when her cell phone rang. She looked at the number but did not recognize it. Maybe it had something to do with Angel or Aaron.

"Hello?" she said.

"Um, hi. I just wanted to make sure you gave me the right phone number. Uh, this is mine, so you should save it in your phone. Goodnight, my love!"

Then the phone went dead. My love? Who did Joe think he was calling her that ridiculous name? She wanted to be mad but was surprised that she was grinning. Goofy Joe actually brought a smile to her face. She had really fallen in rank now that she was looking forward to a date with a geek, but at least Joe would be a good distraction. Ruby threw her head back and laughed hysterically at the entire situation.

"Hey, cabby," she said as one of her favourite songs came on the radio. "Turn the music up because I feel like dancing right now."

Something told her things were going to get interesting and she intended to enjoy every minute of it.

Twenty Five † Brandon

Brandon stiffened a bit as Dana snuggled closer to him in the movie theatre. His original plan was dinner and a movie, and then a fun-filled night with Dana in bed. She was a cute little number who worked in the customer service branch of his company and they had met at a work function. Now that the dinner was out of the way and the movie was ending, Brandon did not feel like taking her home anymore. He was just physically attracted to her and the company they were employed by was the only thing they had in common. Actually, these criteria made her the perfect candidate for a one-night stand but Brandon was not interested.

It had been four months since Brandon met with Karl and decided that Karl could not help him fix his situation. Taking matters into his own hands, Brandon tried to accept that closing the door on Aaron altogether and dating other woman was the best solution. After numerous first dates, nobody seemed worthy of a second date. Being a man, he had needs, but none of these women made him want to break his new record of abstinence. He needed to find someone soon to help him in this area or he would burst.

After the movie, when they got up to leave, Dana again nestled against his body. Her eyes were glazed over with lust and Brandon was very familiar with the unspoken message she was sending him. He just was not in the mood to receive it.

"So, baby, what else do you have on the agenda for tonight?" she asked suggestively, letting her hand slide down his back until it rested on his backside.

Brandon had to use all his strength to stop himself from flinching knowing this action would give Dana the wrong impression. He did not need any false rumours about his sexuality being spread around the office.

"Honestly, Dana, I feel a crazy migraine coming on. I tried to ignore it during the movie but it's really starting to bother me. I'm going to call it a night," he said and kissed her gently on the top of her head.

She did not hide her disappointment and jutted out her bottom lip.

"I'll come back home with you and take care of you, sweetie. I'll be your private nurse," she purred.

Brandon shook his head.

"No, baby. We'll pick up where we left off another time but for now, I need to get home and be in the dark."

He held the movie theatre door for her and guided her out to his car. Any chance for decent conversation was lost because Dana was furious. She moved over as far as possible, making sure that there was no possibility of any physical contact. Brandon was relieved but understood her feeling of rejection. At least he did not sleep with her and then reject her. When he pulled up to her townhouse, she barely said bye as she jumped out and slammed his door. He waited until she was safely inside and then pulled away from the curb.

Four months later and still no worthy companion, he thought. Brandon sighed with a longing so deep he was sure Aaron felt it wherever she was. To make matters worse, he had to go home to his empty home that reminded him so much of her. Her colour schemes, furniture choices and even her belongings were still at his home because, although he intended to, he still had not dropped her stuff to the Goodwill charity box. He knew that parting with her stuff would bring him much needed closure but he was not ready to finalize his loss. To stay away from the house, Brandon managed to throw himself into his job during work hours and appreciated any available overtime he could get. He did not need the money but at least it gave him something to do.

Brandon's cell phone rang, startling him. Now that he isolated himself from everything, he stopped getting regular calls from his buddies to go partying on the weekends. He was not used to hearing the ring after work hours.

"Hello?"

"Hey, what's up, B? It's Karl. How you doing?"

Brandon was shocked to hear from Karl. Their last meeting had been tense and although he missed Karl's friendship and wanted to reach out to him, his pride had stood in the way. Brandon knew he had acted like a wimpy little boy and was embarrassed about the way he treated his friend. Karl was not to blame for his miserable life.

"I'm alright, I guess. What's up?" he asked.

"I'm being recognized at my church for ten years of serving the community and I would feel honoured to have you there as my guest."

Brandon winced at the thought of sitting through a boring presentation but was pleased with any opportunity to bridge the gap between them.

"Sure," he said. "Just tell me when and what time and I'll be there."

"It's this Sunday at my church. They will be doing the presentation during the eleven-thirty service. I'll text you all the details because I'm not sure if you still have the program I gave you."

Brandon felt ashamed as he thought about how quickly he had rolled down his window and tossed the program to the wind in his fit of rage. He could not believe how childish he had acted that day.

"I would appreciate the text. Thanks for inviting me, Karl, and congrats," Brandon said.

"Brandon?"

"Yeah?"

"Has your situation changed at all?" Karl asked

Brandon softened at the concern in his friend's voice. Karl did care, even though Brandon had convinced himself otherwise.

"No, Karl, nothing has changed," Brandon admitted to his friend.

"Well then, I will continue praying for you. Have a blessed night," he said.

"Thanks, Karl, bye."

Brandon did not understand why but he felt a bit of solace in knowing that Karl would *continue* to pray for him. That meant that he was praying for him all this time. Karl really had his back and Brandon felt renewed by the fact that he would be able to repair at least one relationship in his life.

Who knew, maybe he would actually enjoy going to church and find something else to fill the void in his life. He had a decent singing voice and maybe he could join the choir. At least it would give him something more in common with Karl.

Brandon thought about the peaceful nature Karl had about him and longed for that kind of life. Karl was a married man, with two children, and a successful career. Brandon had met Karl's family and he was truly a lucky man. He hoped some of Karl's principles would rub off on him. Brandon was no dummy. He knew he had a successful career and was well to do in life, but that was not the be all and end all for happiness. Brandon wanted a life partner. Maybe he would hook up with a nice, down to earth church girl. The more he thought about it, the more excited he became. Brandon could not believe he was actually looking forward to going to church. What a place for possibilities it was suddenly becoming!

Twenty Six † Aaron

It has been four months since I gave my life to God and everything seems to be falling into place. It turns out that Mrs. Donovan is a long-time member of the church and was ecstatic when she witnessed me being saved. She told me she could not stop crying and came over to embrace me shortly after.

I met with the counselor after service and over the course of a few weeks; I gave him every single detail I could remember from every traumatic experience I ever endured. During the first session, there was also a woman in the room who was an intercessor for the church and they both listened silently as I spoke. To my surprise, they placed their hands on me and prayed. They also thanked God for his mercy and love, and carrying me through every path in my life. They made me feel like my trials and tribulations were positive. Going to the counselor and telling him my experiences seemed to erase them from my being. It is almost as if they happened to someone else. God is so good!

My old apartment held too many memories and secrets that I really did not want to be around anymore. I leased it out and have moved to a quiet residential area. The old place now brings in a regular income that helps with many essentials in life. Carmen is the only person from my past who I still keep in contact with. Despite our age difference, she has become one of my closest friends and is like a little sister to me.

I have a praise report. Another miracle is that Angel is finally home with me again. Mrs. Donovan vouched for me and deemed me a fit parent. She has to visit with me on a monthly basis, which is protocol. But I welcome her into my home anytime—whether the visit is official or not.

I have even been taking part-time courses during the day that count towards a certificate that will be equivalent to a high school diploma, and Children's Aid has arranged childcare for me. The organization has actually turned out to be a helpful resource tool. What I love the most are all of the courses my church offers, some of which are not even directly centered on Christianity. I took a ten-step business start-up course and have completed my business plan. I have decided to go forward with my company and I am currently taking an online course for certification in interior decorating. This certification, partnered with my natural talent, is the equation for success. I also joined the decorating committee at church as it is in the process of moving to a new location, and needed volunteers to plan and decorate the new facilities. The new church has a more modern exterior and has tripled in size. Although it will not be ready for another year, we have already started picking colours, fabric and furniture. I love that the church considers this serving. I feel like I am the one being served.

Because of all these changes, I have become a better mother to Angel—one she can be proud of. The parenting course really informed me about her needs and development, and we spend a lot more quality time together. Our time apart taught her more independence, and I love to watch her interact with other toddlers in her pre-school programs. Angel is smart and does things other children her age cannot yet do. Teachers and instructors are always pointing this out to me.

The only part of my life that feels empty is the hole left by Brandon's absence. I have often entertained the idea of reaching out to him but realize how unfair that would be. I walked out of his life. I shut him out. The least I can do is let him move on in peace. It could not have been easy for him. I was mean and self-centered in the way I treated him. I did not thank him properly for taking care of Angel when I was in the hospital. I hope that one day he can forgive me. Brandon was a part of my life before Jesus, and I know I have to leave him behind and move on. It just sucks that I feel like I will never get over him. I miss the way he smiled, the way he laughed, the smell of peppermint gum on his breath, the quirky faces he would make to get me to laugh. But most of all, I miss the way he loved both Angel and me. I include him in my morning, afternoon and nightly prayers. Above all else, I want Brandon to be happy. He is a good man who treated me like a normal person even before I was saved. With all my heart, I want him to find the right woman and have the family he desires. He deserves it.

Thoughts of Brandon bring tears to my eyes and I do not want Mrs. Donovan to think something is wrong. I am sitting in a booth at Wendy's as she walks towards me, waving. She greets me with a big hug and a peck on the cheek. Since we have become close, she has called me her adopted daughter and welcomed me many times into her home, which she shares with her husband and teenage son.

"So, are you all prepared for service this weekend?" she asks as she slides into the booth across from me.

She never fails to wow me with all the work she does for the church, the effort she puts into her career, and how she still manages to be a good wife and a mom. Mrs. Donovan is head of the volunteer committee at church and has asked me to help at this weekend's service. It is going to be a big one and they need all available hands to help because some of the regular volunteers are being honoured so they will not be able to serve. My role is to intercede when the pastor does an altar call. It turns out that I am gifted with prayer and I am able to go to our Father on other women's behalf. When I am praying for them, I find a voice is telling me just what to say to bring comfort to the person. I cherish this gift and welcome any opportunity to use it.

"I sure am," I reply cheerfully to Mrs. Donovan's question. "It will be my first time serving at an altar call but I am so excited for the opportunity. God is making me flex my spiritual muscles as he continues to use me."

Mrs. Donovan smiles at me as she bites into her Baconator cheese burger. She is the closest thing to a mother as I will ever have and she is perfect. She urges me to forgive my parents and seek them out one day, but I am still learning to forgive. Everything takes time and I am taking baby steps. I do want to forgive them and release us all from this burden. I have learned that God loves them too and wants to give them a new life as well.

Another person who continually pops into my mind is Ruby. I pray for her as well and wish her absolutely no harm. Ruby was good to me and took care of me for many years. Even though I know she meant for me to be harmed, everything worked out in my favour. My gut also tells me it was Ruby who called Children's Aid. But if she had not, I would probably never have ended up going to church and you know the rest of the story. Ruby has hidden pain as well. Although she never shared her story with me, I know something terrible happened to her. I hope that one day I can be a witness to Ruby of God's love and be there to rescue her like she rescued me. I pray she will be led to Jesus so she can be free of the burdens of her past.

"How is our beloved little Angel doing today?" Mrs. Donovan asks.

I love how she calls her "our" Angel. She is more like a grandmother than a caseworker to Angel, and I smile at how strong their connection is.

"She is great. You know Angel," I say with a grin. "I am still baffled at how she answers 'Jesus' when you ask her who her best friend is. I was telling your hubby the other day and he said she is abundantly blessed."

"I know she sings the song, *Jesus, You're My Superhero*, in class but the way she puts things together is beyond me!" Mrs. Donovan replies as she pushes a french fry into her mouth.

Tony is Mrs. Donovan's husband, and he is one of the sweetest, kindest men— ever. He still holds his wife's hand after twenty-four years of marriage, continues to open doors for her and treats her respectfully. He is clearly in awe of his wife and speaks highly of her every chance he gets.

We finish our meal and take a minute to thank God for the wonderful food He provided. After a short but welcome embrace, we leave the restaurant and agree that we're both looking forward to Sunday's service. As I drive home, I realize more than ever that it is time to put some of my thoughts into action. When I get home, I am going to make a list of people and things that need my attention. Our pastor has preached about the power of words and speaking things into our lives. She—yes, the lady at the altar on the day I was saved is the pastor—is very serious about life and death being in the power of the tongue, and I want to make a list of goals I want to accomplish by the end of the following year.

At the top of my list is a letter to Brandon. He deserves to know that Angel and I are well, and I want to invite him to church. Even if he does not come, I want to invite him in faith that God will somehow bring him. If God could bring someone like me to church, it is obvious everyone is welcome. I chuckle as I remember the word the pastor gave on the day I was saved. A prostitute was welcomed into the Kingdom. The message was clear. I wonder what message she will have for Ruby or Brandon if they come around. I know they will show up one day because I walk by faith and not by sight. They both deserve the life that God purposed for them and I would love to see them get everything they truly need.

Twenty Seven † Ruby

Ruby stood outside of her apartment, tapping her foot impatiently as she waited for Joe to pull up. This dude was always late and after four months of dating she thought she would be used to it. She promised herself that this time she would stay angry with him. She gave in too easily and was convinced this was the reason he kept doing it. She had to punish him for being tardy.

Exactly fifteen minutes late, Joe pulled up to the curb and barely put his car into park before flying out to smother her in a warm embrace.

"So sorry I'm late, beautiful, I got stuck in traffic again!" Joe said as he covered Ruby's cheeks and neck with tender kisses.

"Back up off me," Ruby said trying to pull away but knowing that she was setting herself up for failure. "Leave me alone Joe, I'm pissed off."

He responded by kissing her more and hugging her tighter, and she knew she was not successful at punishing him, yet again. She gave in, threw her arms around his neck and planted a juicy kiss on his lips.

So much had changed since she started dating Joe. At first, things were a bit awkward and forced but she kept agreeing to see him out of sheer boredom. She soon found herself falling for him. To her, Joe was no longer goofy—he was just unique, loving and caring. In other words, he had all the qualities she needed in a partner. Joe was a light at the end of her dark tunnel and made her feel important. Ruby loved the way Joe exhibited his masculinity with her when he felt like she needed to be calmed down. He was not the wimp she thought he was. It turned out he was just really shy. The real Joe was strong, authoritative and very accomplished. He told Ruby that he did not want her roaming the streets anymore and he would take care of her, but she was not fully ready to hang up her pimp hat. In the meantime, Ruby was saving money so she could walk away from the streets and be independent since she did not have any other talents or skills and all she knew was the hustle. If one day Joe decided that he wanted someone else, she had to be able to survive on her own. If everything worked out as planned, she would be able to retire in approximately two years so Joe would have to be patient until then.

When they finally pulled away from each other, Joe stepped back and gave her an approving once-over accompanied by a playful whistle.

"You look hot, baby." he said with that look in his eyes, which always led to long nights of lovemaking, cuddling and whispering.

Joe was certainly skilled in bed. Ruby had continued to lose weight and was surprised at the attention her new shape received. She even grew her short hair and wore a more feminine hairstyle. Tonight, she wore a black turtleneck, mini skirt and flat knee-length leather boots. A necklace Joe had given her complimented her complexion and drew attention to her bright blue eyes. Joe was constantly talking about their future children and how they were destined to be beautiful thanks to the combination of both of their features. She always brushed off this type of conversation but was not opposed to having a baby—one day—just not anytime soon.

Ruby loved the way Joe made her feel and wondered for the millionth time if this was how Aaron felt with Scar. She now understood the power of love but would never admit that to Joe because she was afraid he would take advantage of her heart. She refused to make herself vulnerable.

"Thanks, boo," she said using the cuddly pet name she gave him but only used when they were alone because she only felt comfortable expressing affection in private. "You don't look bad yourself."

Joe had on dark jeans and a black tee with a bow tie screen-printed on the front. Since they had become closer, Joe mixed his own style with what he thought would gain Ruby's approval. Secretly, she loved him whether he was nerdy or suave.

She craved Joe's touch more than anything as she thought about how much she loved him, and was willing to call off their plans and just take him upstairs.

"Boo, you sure you want to go out? We could go upstairs and watch movies and get our freak on," she suggested with hope in her eyes.

"We have all night for that, sweetie. I think you're going to enjoy our date tonight. Let's go!" he said, directing her to the passenger side door of the car and helping her in before heading to the driver's side.

This type of gesture used to bother Ruby because she could open her own door. Now, she understood his need to treat her like a lady and allowed herself to enjoy it. She truly felt feminine with him and she rather liked it.

Ruby always looked forward to the date ideas Joe came up with because they never failed to contain a mixture of surprise and excitement. He had taken her to art exhibitions (which she loathed) and museums (which she loved). They had gone to a few concerts and, of course, dinners and movies. Each restaurant was different and he had even sat through girly type of movies with her. She would never admit it, but she enjoyed romantic movies. During these movies she pretended to be the main character and often got lost in the romance of the scenes. She even found herself surfing for black and white movies on television after realizing old Hollywood did romance best.

Joe headed east on the highway and Ruby wondered where he was taking her. All the fun and exciting places were in the opposite direction.

"Um, where are we going?" she asked.

She admired the way Joe shifted gears when he drove. There was something extra sexy about a man who could handle a standard car. It made him seem in control of the world.

"You'll see, baby. Relax," he answered, flashing a quick smile.

"Whatever." she said dismissing him and pulling out her BlackBerry to play *Brick Breaker*. She was determined to beat her reigning high score and gave it her full attention.

Thirty minutes later, they were off the highway and pulling into the parking lot of a park. Ruby looked around and wondered what they were doing here. She turned to ask Joe but he quickly cut her off.

"Don't worry, baby. Sometimes you just gotta trust me."

Ruby hated when he read her mind. This was not the first time he knew exactly what she was going to say before she had a chance to voice her thoughts. It was scary how quickly they had become so connected. Sometimes she felt like it was her need to have someone to call her own. She went over many of Aaron's stories about her relationship with Scar in her head. She had secretly envied what they had and wanted that for herself.

"Fine. It better be good." she said.

Joe got out the car, came around, and opened her door. They walked down a path that started at one end of the parking lot and led them deeply into the forest's paved paths. It was a beautiful nature walk but at first Ruby felt annoyed. Walking along the path with no destination seemed pointless but she eventually relaxed and started to enjoy the beauty around her.

The tall trees and mossy grounds that were now covered with a light blanket of frost were a sight to see. The scene engulfed both sides of the pathway and created an intimate setting. They walked for about ten minutes before coming up to a more open area with gardens, antique iron benches and pedestal water fountains. Ruby was surprised at all the couples strolling along, hand in hand, as well as parents and children. But what stopped Ruby in her tracks was a beautiful bride being photographed with her bridesmaids. She was stunning in a white mink, waist-length coat that complimented her dress. The magical backdrop only added to what Ruby could only imagine was her perfect day.

Ruby felt a stirring in her tummy of want, need and yearning all combined. Could she ever be a bride? Would she ever have what it takes to be a wife? Joe must have read her mind again because he put his arm around her shoulders and pulled her close.

"When we get married, Ruby, I want to come here and take our pictures. You are going to make me a beautiful bride."

Joe's words caught Ruby totally off guard and she was actually speechless. She wanted to argue and tell him she had no desire to ever become a wife because it was not in her DNA but no words came to her lips. Instead, she sighed aloud and rested her head on Joe's shoulder as he dropped his arm and put it around her waist. When she glanced up, Joe had his eyes closed and seemed to be meditating. Ruby had seen him do this many times and was now used to it, but she remembered how uncomfortable it made her the first time she witnessed it. She never asked him why he did it. She figured he must have taken karate or something when he was small and used meditation as his way of finding peace. Today though, she needed to know exactly what he was meditating about since he chose to do it now. When he opened his eyes, she asked him.

"Joe, why do you meditate so much? Are you trying to focus your chakras?" She remembered the word from a yoga DVD that she once watched but never actually did.

"I'm not meditating, Ruby. I'm praying," he said.

"Praying?" she asked a little taken aback. "You mean to God?"

"Yes baby, to God," Joe answered softly.

Ruby laughed. She hated to be the one to have to disappoint Joe when she let him know that God did not exist. If anyone should know, it was she. She used to believe too, thanks to the fairy tales her grandmother read to her from the Bible when she was small. But when it was time for God to show up in her life and help her, He failed and the baby sister she prayed for was taken away so quickly after her birth. If God existed, he had a twisted sense of humour.

"There is no such thing as God," Ruby said, completely sure of herself. "You're wasting your time."

She freed herself from his embrace and started to walk back towards the path, hoping to signal that the conversation was over. She did not want to stir up sad memories of her past. Something about this atmosphere in the park had her all soft and vulnerable, and she did not like it.

"Ruby," Joe said in a concerned tone as he caught up and fell in line with the pace of her now swift footsteps, "what's wrong?"

Ruby could not help herself and did not know why she had a need to vent her anger with God to Joe. This was a protected part of her past that up until now, she did not share with anyone.

"You want to know what's wrong? I'll tell you what's wrong. God is a sick joke that someone started years ago to fool people into believing in someone or something that does not exist to make themselves feel better about life. God gives false hopes, dreams and promises!"

Joe reached out and grabbed her arm halting her pace. Ruby writhed her arm trying to shake free of his grip but was unsuccessful. With an unexpected wave of tears and a scowl on her face, she turned to face him.

"Let me go, you stupid freak. Let go of my arm right now!" she screamed.

A couple walking along the path quickly shuffled past them as the man ushered the woman protectively and glanced at them over his shoulder. Joe pulled Ruby in close and wrapped his arms around her. He was determined not to let her go until she was okay. Ruby stiffened at first and then relaxed at the familiar warmth of his arms. With sweet surrender, she relaxed her whole body against his and let him comfort her.

"Baby, whatever it is that is bothering you, you can talk to me about it. I love you and hate to see you like this," he said.

Ruby used the comfort of his embrace to give her strength to open up to Joe. She never told anyone about her past but knew she had to tell him. She needed to share her grief with someone she could trust. Joe relaxed his hold on her and gently kissed the top of her head, wordlessly encouraging her.

"He took my baby away, Joe, and she was all I had. He let her die!" she sobbed.

"Who took your baby?" Joe said.

He tried to pull away so he could look Ruby in her eyes. But wanting to avoid eye contact, she pulled in closer to him, rested her head on his chest and tightened her arms around his waist.

"God did!" she said and started to weep openly. "God took my baby sister away and left me with nothing. He did not protect her, Joe, and I prayed and prayed and prayed and prayed."

Joe rubbed Ruby's back waiting for her to keep talking. She poured out her pain and anguish into Joe's chest, only stopping to take much-needed deep breaths or to wipe her now runny nose on the handkerchief he had given her. As she finished telling her story so did her tears stop flowing, her shoulders stopped violently shaking and the rhythm of her breathing returned to normal. Ruby pulled away from Joe and bowed her head to wipe away any traces of tears that were left over from her breakdown. She was too embarrassed to look at him but his silence was tormenting her. She slowly turned to him slowly.

"You think I'm a freak now, don't you?" she inquired. "A big loser freak with a freaky childhood to match."

Joe tilted her face up to his but his eyes did not say anything negative. There was a mixture of empathy, concern and love vibrating from the core of his soul.

"Baby, you are not a freak and nothing in this whole entire world would ever make me think that about you. I love you. You need to know something though," he said taking both of Ruby's hands into his and pulling them to his lips for a kiss. "What happened to your baby sister was not your fault or God's. He loves you and would never do anything to make you sad."

"Then why..."

"I don't know why that tragedy happened to you and your sister. I wish I had answers for you. It sucks that you had to endure all that pain by yourself for so long, but no more, baby. God loves you, and so do I," Joe said and kissed her openly and fervently.

Ruby was overcome by the depth of his love and started to feel a little uncomfortable with it.

Everything she loved seemed to leave her. She loved and lost her grandmother, her sister and Aaron; what if she lost Joe, too? She pulled away and took a step back.

"Enough with this God talk," she said, adding a little giggle to make her statement sound casual. "I'm ready to go and finish off our night."

Ruby started heading back up the path but stopped when she did not feel Joe's presence behind her. She turned around to see Joe in the same spot she left him but on his knee. Ruby knew what he was doing because she lived this moment with him before. Except this time, she loved him. After everything she told him, he still wanted her to be his wife. Either Joe was desperate or he really, truly loved her. Ruby walked slowly back to him with all the love and compassion her heart could hold.

"Ruby Damco, I love you and need you in my life forever. You are beautiful inside and out, and I knew the first day I met you that you were the one for me. Baby, will you be my wife?" Joe held out the same ring he presented to her the first time he had asked for her hand in marriage.

Ruby knew her answer right away but had to make Joe understand she was whom she was and was not going to change.

"I will, Joe, but you need to understand that I can't change who I am and you will have to love me for who I am and..."

Joe jumped up, kissed Ruby passionately on the lips cutting her off mid-sentence, and then lifted her off the ground and spun her around. He placed the antique looking ring, which Ruby would later find out belonged to his great grandmother, on her finger. Ruby laughed with him as they embraced, kissed and skipped up the pathway. Joe made a point of telling anyone who passed them that Ruby said *yes*, and instead of being annoyed, she felt honored and excited. With all her baggage and shortcomings, Joe still wanted her as his wife. This was something to celebrate. Ruby finally had someone to love who would love her right back forever and ever. Who knows, she thought, maybe, just maybe, there is a God!

Twenty Eight † Brandon

It was Sunday morning, the day of the presentation that Karl had invited Brandon to, and Brandon stood staring at his closet, wishing that a suitable outfit would jump out of the closet and dress him. He had absolutely no idea what to wear. It was during times like this when he longed for the right woman to settle down with. She would know what Brandon should wear. He knew whom the right woman was but refused to say or even think her name, knowing that relationship was over. He still missed her and wondered when the pain would fade. They said time healed a broken heart but he felt the opposite as the pain and longing for her and Angel had intensified as the weeks went by. This really was not normal.

He sighed and again gazed at the rows of business suits, button-downs and T-shirts, jeans, and khakis that filled his closet. Nothing seemed right. The suits were too dressy and the street clothes were too casual. In the end, Brandon decided to dress business-casual and selected a dark pair of nicely fitted denim jeans, a dark dress shirt minus the tie and his argyle sweater vest. He completed the outfit with his chestnut brown, three-quarter length leather jacket that was lined with Merino wool, which he received as a present from his mother last Christmas. He saved this jacket for special occasions and seeing his friend being honoured was definitely that.

Brandon decided to go ahead with his plan to keep his eyes open for a nice woman in church. He went over to the vanity counter in his bathroom to select cologne that was nice but not overbearing, and chose the Jean Paul Gaultier one that Aaron had surprised him with to celebrate their third month together. He loved the scent and anytime he had worn it, Aaron had found it hard to drag her nose away from his body. Although it brought back memories of her, he sprayed it on as a good luck fragrance to entice other women.

All he wanted was the opportunity to mend his heart, move on and fall in love with someone else. Brandon had not given up on the idea of falling in love again and it was actually the only thing carrying him right now. He no longer got pleasure from the simple things he used to adore like watching sports, hanging with friends or clubbing.

In the moment he still had fun but as soon as the activity or event was over, so was his good mood.

Brandon rolled his eyes at himself in the mirror. He could not believe how pathetic and woeful he had become over the last few months. He needed to man up and move on but truly did not know how. Something told him, or maybe he just convinced himself, that today there was going to be a breakthrough. He was going to use the principles he learned from the self-help book, *The Secret*, to align his thoughts with the universe. From skimming the book, he remembered that you had to act and believe that things would happen. Therefore, the cologne was his way of saying, "I am a woman magnet and today I will attract that right girl to me."

By the time he climbed into his car, Brandon's mood had lightened and he allowed himself to take comfort in that. After double-checking the text message Karl had sent him with directions to the church, he set off. As he drove with music playing softly, Brandon toyed with the idea of *The Secret*. What kind of woman would he manifest into his life? She definitely needed to be curvy because he liked his woman to have meat on their bones but in terms of looks, he could not think of anything specific. If he could, he would duplicate Aaron's looks but obviously that was impossible. Besides, he admitted, he did not want a woman whose looks reminded him of Aaron. He adored her personality so much that he knew even someone who resembled her would pale in comparison.

Meeting someone who was very different from her was his best plan of action.

After a few agonizing minutes filled with memories of Aaron, he decided to focus on something else and turned his thoughts to Karl. He wondered where Karl found the time to balance family, work and service to his church. Ten years was a long time to volunteer and he knew Karl did not half-ass anything. He would never say this out loud but he also wondered what satisfaction Karl felt from working in the church. He was not paid and yet he dedicated so much time. Brandon just did not understand that.

Twenty-five minutes later, he pulled into the church parking lot and admired the mixture of high-end and average cars. He was not sure what he expected but certainly not what was in front of him. He was glad his Mercedes-Benz did not stick out like a sore thumb and made a mental note to ask Karl who drove the sexy Jaguar parked at the front of the church. His watch read five minutes after eleven so Brandon took the time to sit back and watch people going into the church. He noticed many families with children and admired the women who walked in alone. He had not really expected to see so many attractive women but they were definitely present. He silently thanked the universe for giving him a wonderful flock of options. Knowing that he was an attractive man with a magnetic personality, Brandon looked forward to working his game in church.

Brandon made his way into the church, thinking it was a nice looking building. The exterior made it seem stuffy but he could tell the interior had been renovated from the original blueprint. After being greeted by the ushers at the front, Brandon entered the main auditorium. He immediately saw Karl talking and laughing with a few well-dressed men. They made eye contact and Karl motioned him over with a wave.

"Hey, how are you doing, Brandon? I'm so happy you came," Karl said.

He gave Brandon a friendly pat on the back then immediately started introducing him to his circle of friends. He was happy that he decided to come until, much to his hesitation, Karl signaled for Brandon to follow him to the front of the church. He would have felt better in the back, where he would not have hundreds of eyes burning in the back of his head.

"Yeah, um, Karl, I'm just going to take a seat back here," he said.

"Nonsense. You are my guest, and I really want you to sit up front in the row reserved for my family and friends. Don't worry, I'm not going to do anything to embarrass you," Karl replied, acknowledging his friend's discomfort.

"Okay. Fine," Brandon agreed not wanting to make a big issue out of nothing.

He noticed that some of the other men were looking at him and he did not want to appear a coward to any of his new acquaintances. Besides, what could really happen?

When they reached the row reserved for Karl's family and friends, Brandon greeted Karl's wife, Denise, who was already seated. She stood and he kissed her formally on both cheeks.

"Thanks for coming to celebrate with Karl," she said. "He was really hoping that you would. It means the world to him." She smiled and sat back down.

Brandon made himself comfortable in his seat, which was not the expected oak pew that you typically saw in churches, but a padded stackable chair. Brandon leaned closer to Karl, who was seated next to him.

"Nervous?"

"Not nervous but excited." Karl answered.

"Well, I know that you work hard. You're more than deserving." Brandon said.

"I'm not sure about the deserving part, Brandon, but I am honoured to be recognized. We can never give enough of ourselves to others. Jesus Christ gave his life for us so I'm grateful to be able to give back some of myself," he replied, before whispering, "There's the praise and worship leader."

He stood as the band started to play and a woman made her way to centre stage. Again, Brandon was thrown by how humble Karl was as he stood up as well.

"Welcome, everybody. Today is going to be a special day so please join me as we clap to the Lord and give Him all the praise and glory," said the worship leader as she began to clap and shuffle side to side to the beat of the drums.

Now, this, Brandon could get into. According to his parents, Brandon was born with such rhythm that he practically danced his way out of his mom's womb. He easily fell into the gentle clap and shuffle routine, which was shortly followed by the beginning of a gospel song. Although he was no Luther Vandross, Brandon knew that if T-Pain could make music, he could sing too. The songs were easy to sing along with since the words were projected on a big on-stage screen. Brandon was having so much fun with the upbeat songs that he caught smiles from a few women around him. He found the words to the songs uplifting, and felt more alive and free than he had in a long time. It must have been the first time since the break-up that Aaron did not cross his mind. Karl gave Brandon a friendly pat on the back and encouraged him to keep enjoying himself. As Brandon quickly turned around and scanned the room, it seemed like everyone was having a good time too.

After five quick songs, they shifted to a slow and moving beat. Everyone immediately slowed their steps and some swayed, while others stood perfectly still. There were arms stretched towards the ceilings as the beat came through the speakers from the hands of the gifted band members. Brandon caught himself staring at the drummer who seemed to be lost in his own world. He admired the expressiveness that flowed from his drumsticks.

Two men with a protective demeanour led a beautiful woman onto the stage. Her beauty captivated Brandon but it was not the kind of beauty you would see in a magazine. There was something about her that glowed and as she looked around the auditorium, her eyes were filled with love. The words for the next song appeared on the screen and holding the mic, she sang along with the congregation. She was no Jennifer Hudson but her voice held a sweet sincerity. Brandon could tell she not only enunciated the words of the song but she also believed them. He was thrown by the emotion he felt stirring as he stood still and did his best to follow along with the song. A harmony filled the room that fueled him with a want and need for more. He felt a blanket of love, which was silently shared with each and every person present, covering the room. Feeling safe, he wanted to stay in this very place and moment forever.

After the singing ended, the pastor said a short prayer, blessing everyone, and asked them to be seated. Brandon stared straight ahead in fear that Karl or the man next to him would notice his misty eyes. Now that the singing had stopped, he had better control over his emotions and did not know what had happened to him. He was a bit embarrassed but realized no one was paying attention to him. Everyone was engrossed in what the pastor was saying.

"...if you want something in your life to change, ask yourself: Does something need to change or do I need to change something?" Her eyes scanned the room. "The Israelites went around the same mountain for forty years because of this very reason. God set them free from being enslaved under the pharaoh's rule in Egypt, and instead of obeying and being thankful, they bickered, complained and sinned. How many of you are so caught up in what you don't have that you can't see how blessed you truly are? Will you continue to circle the same mountain or will you change something?"

Like a lightning bolt, her message ripped through Brandon and spoke straight to his heart. He was so busy feeling sorry for himself about losing two relationships that he never looked inwardly. He suddenly felt like a fool for moping these last couple of months, and compromising his work ethic and relationships with the friends he continually brushed off. This was a perfect example of him not embracing the good in his life.

"...our Lord and Saviour came to set us free. All pity we feel for ourselves is foolishness. If something in your life needs to change, change it. Jesus said in Mark 11:22 to have faith in God. Say to that mountain, without any doubt in your heart, 'Be removed in the name of Jesus' and what you say will happen." She stopped pacing to stare deeply into the faces in the audience. "Do you need to move a mountain today? What is your mountain?"

She continued walking back and forth on the stage.

"Is your mountain your finances? Is it your credit? Is it being stuck in the same abusive relationship year after year? Is your mountain drugs or alcohol? Whatever your mountain is, have faith in God and move it!" she said in a strong, authoritative voice.

Her message touched the congregation and was celebrated with shouts of "Amen!" and "Praise God!" echoing throughout the room. Brandon nodded his head in appreciation. He really meditated on what she was saying.

"In order to celebrate people who are moving mountains and living purpose-driven lives, I would like to call up Sharon for a special presentation," she said.

Brandon felt Karl's body straighten up beside him in anticipation of what was coming. This was the moment he was waiting for, and Brandon was really excited and proud of Karl.

After the reason for the awards was shared, five men including Karl were called up on stage and their families were told to join them. Seeing Karl beaming on stage made Brandon take a minute to re-evaluate his life. As the emcee listed all of Karl's accomplishments from the last ten years, Brandon felt foolish about the thoughts he had beforehand. So what if Karl did not get paid? This reward was worth more than money. Seeing the presentation also made Brandon yearn for more as he realized he wanted to make a difference in someone's life.

The honourees returned to their seats after shaking the hands of everyone in the front row and receiving friendly pats on the back. Brandon felt like a proud papa and the friend of a celebrity from all the love and attention that was being directed at Karl. He was glad he was sitting next to his friend.

The pastor continued her sermon and touched on many things in Brandon's life that needed to be addressed. He was relating to everything she was saying so much that he could not believe it was not written just for him. He actually wondered if Karl submitted notes to the pastor and asked her to touch on them.

Thirty minutes later, the pastor concluded her sermon, and the praise and worship team joined her on stage again along with the band. They sang another slow gospel song and once more, Brandon was moved by the power of love and unity that filled the room. This time, he could not help the tears falling from his eyes and wept quietly. A part of him cried pitifully for himself and for all the pain he suffered in the last few months, and another part of him wept because he could not believe that he missed this type of fellowship over the years. He felt like he was born for this day and wanted to belong. Something unseen was pulling at his heart, and when the pastor asked if anyone wanted to receive Jesus Christ as his or her Lord and Saviour, Brandon jumped up without hesitation. Karl stood with him and embraced his friend before following him to the front. Brandon felt more affection than he had felt in months.

He was led to a man who prayed with him and asked him to repeat some passages and words that invited Jesus Christ into his heart as his lord and saviour, and Brandon obeyed. He felt lighter than he had ever felt and as the tears streamed from his eyes for what he was leaving behind and what was yet to come, Brandon lost the feelings in his legs. He was grateful for the hands he felt holding him up and encouraging him with kind words. After a few minutes, Brandon was strong enough to stand on his own. The man who prayed for him congratulated him, embraced him and welcomed him into the Kingdom. Brandon thanked him and turned to return to his seat but became immobile when he found himself standing face to face with an angel.

He fell to his knees with a wave of fresh tears as Aaron stood staring at him. She seemed to be in shock and dropped a box of Kleenex she had been holding to the floor. People around them watched with curiosity. Karl looked back and forth between the two and seemed to understand what was going on, and whom she was. Aaron walked up to Brandon who was still on his knees, pulled his head into her stomach, and held him close as his arms encircled her waist. She then crouched down to his level and held him in her arms. Neither one of them spoke a word as they embraced tightly and let unshed tears flow without inhibition. Yes, Brandon thought, there definitely is a God!

Twenty Nine † Aaron

I cannot believe this day is finally here. All the stress I endured during these last four months since God brought Brandon and me back together has been more than worth it. Besides, it was stress that made me smile since it was caused by fittings, meetings, counseling and preparation for my wedding day.

Since seeing Brandon in the church that day, I often giggle to myself when I think about what a humorous God we serve. I never gave up on love and prayed that God would send me a God-fearing man for my husband. Instead, he sent my husband to church and changed him.

It is only eight in the morning, but as the sound of the doorbell snaps me out of my thoughts I welcome it because I know it is the wedding team that was hired to prepare me for my day. I rush to the door to let in my hair stylist, make-up artist and manicurist. I love that they are all members of our church. The wedding ceremony starts at noon, so I have plenty of time to get ready.

When Carmen, who is my maid of honour, arrives a few minutes after my glam squad, she looks fresh-faced and ready for duty. Her pale yellow, calf-length dress compliments her complexion and makes her radiant. While her hair, which is in a messy bun, perfectly completes her look.

"So, butterflies eating up your belly yet?" Carm asks as she kisses me on the cheek.

"Yes, but it feels so good." I can hardly contain my excited yelps and squeals.

Everyone in the room smiles and giggles with me, and I feel like a queen.

Two hours later, my hair and make-up are done. When I survey myself in the mirror, I have to blink hard so the tears that threaten to spill do not ruin my make-up.

"You look so beautiful! I have only seen people this stunning on the covers of magazines," Carm says as she stares at me in awe.

I cannot stop staring at myself. My hair is coiffed and goes into a ponytail, which falls over my left shoulder. I never knew that my wild hair could be tamed to look so silky and glamorous.

"Thank you," I say to Carm and then turn to my team and hug each one of them. "I absolutely love what you did!"

It is time to put on my dress and the butterflies in my stomach multiply in anticipation. It's hard to put into words how I feel about my dress. When I went to the bridal boutique and tried on dress after dress, I really did not think I would find *the one*. The bridal consultant looked like she was ready to pass out by the time I found it. When I tried it on, I cried and I knew it was *the one* by my reaction.

My dress must have been made with me in mind. It is exactly how I pictured it: halter style with beading from the top to underneath my bosom. The rest of the dress is satin and flows from under my bosom to the end of the earth—at least that's how it feels. It is free flowing but naturally wraps itself around my curves, especially when I walk. It is weird how you can actually love a garment. I cannot wait to see how I look in it now that I am all done up.

My three bridesmaids, whom I met at Bible study, arrive just in time to help me with the finishing touches. They are all dressed in dark yellow ankle length dresses with spaghetti straps and look so pretty. I step into the bathroom, with Carm at my heels, to put on my dress. Having surfed the Internet for a list of maid of honour duties, she has taken her role very seriously and helps me to put on my dress. Once I wiggle into it, she makes me close my eyes and leads me out to the full-length mirror. I am motivated by all the gasps I hear when I re-enter the room. After Carm prompts me, I open my eyes and stand frozen with delight.

Of course I had tried on the dress and knew how it looked, but with the hair, make-up and jewellery, the transformation is remarkable. I stare, wide-eyed, into the mirror and allow myself to bathe in my own splendor. I cannot even pretend to be humble right now as I spin to face my friends.

"Everything is perfect, just perfect! I feel like a movie star!" I say, clapping my hands.

A loud response of encouraging words rings through the room, as everyone begins to compliment me. Carm starts crying and I playfully threaten that if she makes me cry, she is going to get it.

My photographer, who had also arrived earlier to take pictures while I was getting ready, wants me to pose for more photos and the next hour is spent with me acting like a super model. So far, I love each and every minute of this day.

When the doorbell rings, the photo shoot is cut short because Carm tells me that the stretch limo is here to whisk me off to a completely new life. With Carm holding Angel, who, with her extra rosy cheeks, looks like a doll in a white ballerina style dress and puffy ponytail on top of her head, we get set to head out. I am so thankful that Carm got Angel ready so I wouldn't have to worry about it.

"Aaron," says Carm, gently touching my arm, with so much emotion in her voice, "before we go, I want to tell you how privileged I feel to not only be a part of your wedding but to actually be your maid of honour. I love you so much!"

"I love you, too, sweetie. Trust me, I'm the one who's honoured and lucky to have you as my friend," I reply sincerely.

Carm has remained my closest friend even after l left my old life behind, and I'll never forget how she was always on Team Brandon and never bothered to hide her disappointment after our breakup.

"Shall we go then?" asks Carm in a ridiculous account of a British accent as she hands Angel to one of my bridesmaids to grab the train of my dress and help me outside.

"We shall!" I say with an equally funny accent.

As we drive towards the church, my life feels like a dream. When I think about where I started and where I am now, I realize how truly blessed I am. I am fully healed from my past and have God, my church and supportive friends to thank. I know a lot of my healing has to do with Brandon who loves me so unconditionally. To know that I almost lost him...*no words.* He welcomed me back easily and never made me feel bad about how I treated him. He says the time away from me really put his life into perspective and we both know it was part of God's strategic plan for our lives. So many things changed while we were apart and we are now better people for it.

Angel never forgot Brandon and fell back into step with him naturally. When I saw how much he had missed her and how much he loves her, I could not believe I took her away from him so abruptly. My self-pity almost damaged three lives.

The limo seems to float on a cloud and a twenty-minute drive feels like an eternity. When we finally arrive at the church, from the amount of cars in the parking lot, including the Jaguar which belongs to my pastor, I can tell everyone has arrived on time. Despite what I know is a packed church, there is only one person on my mind. I am so anxious to become Mrs. Brandon Conrad, but I am glad my six-inch spiked heels prevent me from bolting out of the car and down the aisle to his arms. That would not be very graceful at all.

My short time in the waiting room seems endless after the bridesmaids and then Carm leave. But I am overcome with joy and peace. The piano starts to play the *Wedding March*, and I know it is time. I have chosen to not have anyone give me away as a substitute for my father but I am okay with that. Those little details do not matter to me. All that matters is that I am marrying Brandon.

As I enter the church and everyone stands, I can feel all eyes lovingly burning into me but I keep my gaze fixed on my Prince Charming waiting for me at the altar. I keep my pace slow and steady as I step over the yellow petals that cover the carpet. I refuse to rush the moment but never take my eyes off Brandon, who returns my intense gaze. This is our time and our spirits seem to make that connection as I ascend towards him. He stands proudly, looking handsome in his tuxedo and pale yellow tie.

When I am almost there, Brandon cannot wait and walks a few short steps forward to take my hand. He stops me in my tracks and lifts my veil over my head as I grin at him.

"Aaron, you look absolutely beautiful and I love you so much," he says and a chorus of awes fills the room. "Let's get married!"

I nod in agreement as he leads me to stand in front of our pastor.

Everyone else in the room vanishes from my sight and I am left alone with my handsome fiancé. Luckily, I seem to know when to speak and what to say, and so does Brandon. His eyes tell me familiar tales and speak of adventures yet to come.

As I say, "I do!" in my boldest voice, I am swept into my husband's arms for a deep kiss. The room starts spinning as I feel as though we are floating towards the ceiling. It is the sound of applause that makes me aware of other people in the church. Brandon lifts me into his arms and carries me out of the church while our loving guests shout out their appreciation and congratulations. Once we get outside, he gently puts me down and pulls me in for another kiss.

"I love you, Mrs. Conrad!" Brandon says giving me the sexiest smile ever.

Yes, I think, I get to have my way with my hubby—at last!

The reception is beautiful. We have rented out the facilities in a five-star hotel and it is breathtaking. The yellow decor is vibrant but stark white hits of colour throughout the room tone it down. Everything sparkles, from the crystal wine glasses to the crystal chandeliers. After a great dinner, our first dance (and then a few more), toasts and mingling with our friends, we sneak away from the celebration and escape to our honeymoon suite. As soon as we step off the elevator, Brandon once again picks me up.

"You don't have to carry me all the way down the hallway," I giggle.

"Oh, yes, I do, Mrs. Conrad," Brandon says. "From now on, I carry you everywhere you go."

"Oh, I can get used to this," I say as I let my head fall back to rest on his shoulder and tighten my arms around his neck.

My heart quickens, as we get closer to our room. Brandon pauses a moment before pulling out the key card for the room.

"Ready, baby?" he asks.

"Ready!" I reply.

I really was not ready though because nothing on earth could have prepared me for the winter wonderland into which Brandon carries me. The absolutely inviting bed is covered with white silk and satin sheets, and an abundance of pillows; crystal decor matches that of the reception hall, beautiful white roses have been placed all over the room in bundles, and a white leather loveseat with fluffy white throw pillows is positioned in front of the electric fireplace, which is made of beautiful mosaic tiles.

Brandon pulls me by the hands in front of the full-size vanity mirror in the bedroom area. I stand facing my reflection as Brandon peers into the mirror over my shoulder. He wraps his arms around me and pulls me tightly into his body as he prays. After we say "amen" in unison, he gently spins me around and plants a wonderful kiss on my lips that makes me feel safe. Brandon transformed so quickly into a true man of God that my recently developed distrust of men had totally vaporized. Because I trust God, I fully trust Brandon.

My husband helps me to carefully take off my delicate wedding dress. I thought I would be sad to remove it, but I am totally okay. After all, my dress is only a material commodity that was used for my wedding, but Brandon is a living, breathing partner who will love me for the rest of my life.

Brandon makes love to me passionately, and it is truly different and was worth the wait. My goal has changed from feeling good to bonding and becoming one. I cry, he cries and we smile. I am his and he is mine. As my husband touches me as his Wife for the first time, I truly lose my virginity. Only our Heavenly Father could have restored my body to undefiled and whole. No longer am I a prostitute, seductress or a sexy being. I am now a woman worthy of being a wife.

"Thank you, Daddy, for redeeming me and loving me through every iniquity," I say to God as I begin to fall asleep. "Thank you for my husband."

Thirty † Ruby

Ruby could not understand the changes that lately had been taking place in her mind. She felt like she was losing who she was but embraced the change at the same time. Joe had her doing and saying things that were totally out of character for her.

Now that she knew what he was doing when he sat in silence with his eyes closed, she had started doing the same. At first, she had just sat there staring at him but after a while, she began closing her eyes too. Praying was weird and a little embarrassing because weird people did that kind of thing. You are talking to yourself and pretending that someone is listening.

Her first few attempts did not go so well. As Joe closed his eyes, she did the same but kept peeking to see if he was watching her and finding humour in what she was doing. After about a week of this, Ruby realized he never looked, and she was free to relax and give it her all. That was when her thoughts during the times Joe prayed started to change. She went from closing her eyes and feeling anxious to finding it peaceful. She would imagine a good life with Joe, real friends around her and just being happy. After three weeks, Ruby started praying as well, hoping that she was being heard.

She would never forget the actual prayer that changed her life. She was by herself at home, snuggled comfortably in a blanket on her couch when thoughts of her baby sister ran through her mind.

"Why now?" she muttered aloud.

She had been so content for so long and memories of her sister were lethal to her emotions. Ruby became so angry for allowing her mind to wander to her sister that she started screaming as a distraction. The scream came from the depth of her belly and felt good being released. She screamed louder and did not care who heard her because it felt too good.

"Screw you, mom, for choosing drugs over your own children! Screw you, dad, for taking off! And a big screw you, grandma, for dying and leaving me alone with her!" Her shouts were interspersed with more screams as she paced the full length of her home. "Screw you, Aaron, for forgetting all I did for you and leaving me behind!" she continued. "Screw you, Joe, for loving me and making me actually care! Screw you, God, for not being there for me when I needed you the most!"

Oh yeah, Ruby thought, this feels so good. She could not stop and, frankly, she did not want to. This conversation was overdue and she was not relenting, no matter what the consequences might be.

"Yeah, I said it," she started up again. "Screw you, *Mr. God*. I was not good enough for you so why should you be good enough for me? Why didn't you let me die as a baby too, huh? Why did you take my sister and not save me by killing me too, huh? What did I do to you to make you hate me so much? Screw you!"

Ruby started to sob, feeling extremely weak and exhausted. She had to sit down and somehow managed to make it back over to her couch. After a little while, she calmed down and used the bottom of her T-shirt to wipe her face. Although she was still angry, Ruby could not understand why she felt guilty for the things she had just said. She was dealt a shitty hand and no amount of prayer or love from Joe was ever going to fix the hole that was in her heart. Ruby closed her eyes and sat quietly, as she had done in the last few weeks. She needed to get to a happy place before she totally self-destructed.

"God," she began, "I'm not sorry for the things I said because they are the truth. If you really existed, you would know that I tell it like it is. However, if you are real and have even an ounce of something for me, can you give me a sign that you are there? I really need something to hold on to right now."

Ruby sat up straight as she heard a soft knock on the door. Nobody came to visit her unannounced and she was not in the mood for company or distractions. She stayed still on her couch hoping the intruder would go away. The knocking, however, became louder. Ruby swore under her breath and got up, ready to rebuke the person who dared to disturb her. She flung open the door and was shocked to see the elder lady who moved next door to her a couple of months ago standing at the door.

"Oh!" the woman said, clearly startled by the aggressive way Ruby opened the door. "Is this a bad time?"

Feeling ashamed of herself, Ruby quickly transformed her attitude to match the stranger's friendly demeanour. She always had a thing for older people.

"Uh, not at all. Can I help you?" Ruby asked, more than a little curious as to why this sweet-looking lady was at her door.

"I've been meaning to come by and introduce myself to you for some time now but I've been pretty busy trying to settle in," she replied. "I was just watching my favourite show and it came to me that now would be a good time to say hello! For some odd reason, you won't stop running through my mind." She laughed quietly.

How weird, Ruby thought. Who randomly goes to introduce themselves to their neighbour?

"Oh," she said, not taking the opportunity to invite in the woman who, after all, was a stranger.

"Well, I'm settled in now and really don't know anyone in the area and thought that maybe you would like to come over for some tea? I have a pot brewing right now and would love if you joined me." She smiled.

Ruby did not know how to respond. Tea? She was not a tea drinker and did not really do this kind of thing. Looking down at her now tear-stained T-shirt and jogging pants, she realized her appearance was not presentable either. She was just about to say so but the woman cut her off.

"Please forgive me for not properly introducing myself. My name is Belinda. I hope I haven't intruded on your privacy," she said.

Ruby felt ashamed for not being polite.

"I'm Ruby. Um, sure, I would love to come for tea," She looked down at her attire, again signaling her discomfort. "I just need to change first then I'll come right over."

"Nonsense! You are just fine. No need to doll yourself up for little old me but I'm flattered," she answered.

"Okay," Ruby relented and reached behind the door for her keys.

She considered bringing her cell phone but changed her mind. She did not really feel like talking to anyone anyway. After locking up, Ruby followed Belinda to her unit and was surprised that she opened the door without the key. Ruby trusted no one and would never leave her door unlocked, not even for a moment.

"Welcome to my home!" Belinda exclaimed as she walked inside, holding the door for Ruby, who was instantly enveloped by coziness and warmth.

Belinda's apartment was traditional, with heavy beige couches, oriental style rugs coloured in warm reds, golds and browns, and collectables that accented the entire place. What a contrast to the modern style of Ruby's apartment. The decor made Ruby think of her grandmother's home. She missed her so dearly. Ruby walked up to a beautiful porcelain doll that was in a glass case situated in the entryway of the apartment. As a child, Ruby always loved porcelain dolls but never got one. Her mom did give her a lot of candy, but toys were not something Ruby received because, as her mom never failed to tell Ruby, she had better things to do with her money.

"I have collected porcelain dolls since my grandmother gave me some when I was small, and have continued into my old age," Belinda giggled.

Ruby smiled and felt a sense of connection to Belinda.

"I always loved them too, but no one ever gave me one when I was a little girl. This one is so pretty."

"Thank you," Belinda paused, clearly unsure of whether she should continue. "I am going to tell you something, but you have to promise not to laugh at me. When I am buying my dolls, I look for the one that talks to me and asks me to take it home. This one came to live with me three years ago. I call her Chantale. "

"Well, she's a beauty," Ruby said.

She followed Belinda over to her small breakfast table. Belinda already had the table set as though she was expecting company and Ruby knew it was for her.

"Biscuit?" Belinda asked as she held the small blue and white china plate out for Ruby to select from.

Ruby smiled and reached for her favorite Peek Frean cookie, which was covered in sugar. She could not remember having one since she was a child when her grandmother used to give them to her. She felt a little sad at the memory and a sharp pain shot through her heart as she thought of the mean things she uttered about her beloved Grandmother during her rampage.

She realized she must have made a sound because Belinda affectionately placed her hand on Ruby's for a second as if to comfort her then reached for a Fruit Crème cookie with cream and jelly in the middle.

"These cookies have all kinds of memories attached to them because they have been around for so many years," she acknowledged. "I used to give them to my grandchildren when they would visit. Now, we live so far away from each other and I miss them dearly."

Ruby was interested in the story and wanted to hear more.

"Oh, you have small grandchildren?"

"Oh, heavens, no," Belinda laughed. "They are grown folks now. Actually, you remind me of my youngest grandbaby. Her name is Amanda and you look to be around her age."

Ruby smiled at Belinda, hoping she would tell her more. Her silence and smile must have been a signal to Belinda as she poured a cup of tea for Ruby and continued her story.

"I have six grandchildren in total. I was blessed with four from my daughter, Mary, who is my eldest child. She has three boys and one girl. My son, who is my youngest, blessed me with two grandchildren, one boy and one girl."

"What a big family!" Ruby said, having always wished she came from one.

She wondered if Joe wanted to have lots of children.

"Oh, not big enough. I always regretted only having two children but my dear husband, God rest his soul, worked so hard to take care of the four of us. Back then, money was harder to come by and raising the two was challenging enough. I realize now that we focused on the wrong things. More children would have been a blessing and our Father would have provided for us no matter how large we grew," she said.

Belinda paused to sip her tea and so did Ruby. She was a little confused by what Belinda said. Who was her father? Since she said 'our father,' Ruby reasoned, she must have been talking about her siblings. Her father had to have been a wealthy man.

"Um, Belinda," Ruby asked, "was your father rich or something? How come he would have provided for you?"

Belinda smiled, lowered her cup and looked Ruby in her eyes as she answered.

"I mean our Heavenly Father, dear. He provides for all his children—you included," she said as if her statement was law before taking another sip of her tea.

Ruby was dumbfounded.

"You mean God?"

"He's the one," Belinda said, smiling. "Oh, He loves us so!"

Ruby could not take it. Why did it seem like lately God was everywhere? First it was Joe, now her sweet neighbour and she was not having it.

"Well Belinda, you might be one of the lucky ones but God doesn't love me. Actually, He can't stand me and I can't stand Him either!" Ruby's matter-of-fact tone came across sharper than she had intended.

Belinda put down her cup, reached across the table and took Ruby's hand.

"My dear child, you are so wrong and I'm sure about this." She released Ruby's hand and continued, "When I was small, I grew up on a farm in Alberta. There were ten children born to my mother and father, rest their souls, and I was somewhere in the middle. We worked hard to tend to the farm and the best time we had was the Sundays when we would set off to church in town. I hated the farm life and felt we were dealt a bad hand because I wanted to be a big star like Marilyn Monroe. Everything we had was a hand-me-down and we worked harder than many other children I knew in school or church. I really despised God back then for giving us the life we had. I could not stand that my parents had so many children. Well, one day when I was supposed to be helping the others clean out one of our barns, I ventured off on a mission of my own. Streams and a small river surrounded our property and I loved being by myself, creating characters, in my imagination, that I wanted to be. To this day, I cannot remember exactly what happened but I found myself slipping into the rushing current of the river and although I was a strong swimmer, the intensity of it was pulling me under. Aside from the strong current, there were sharp rocks imbedded in the river. I thought I was a goner and in desperation, I called out to God for help. I had no other way! Well, wouldn't you know that almost at once I stopped being dragged? My left leg was ensnared in a thick blade of grass and I used all my strength to pull myself to dry ground. After catching my breath and regaining my strength, I thanked God for hearing my prayers and helping me. I have never turned back since. For all the mean and bad thoughts I had about God—I was the only one of us 10 children who openly cursed Him—He still saved me! He could have let me die and freed my parents of such a rebel but He had mercy and love for me, just like He loves all of us," she concluded.

Ruby was mesmerized by Belinda's story but did not feel it applied to her. It only confirmed her original thinking. It was great that God saved Belinda from a tragic death but He had not been as kind to Ruby.

"He never did anything for me," she said. "He gave me a mom who was a drug addict, He stole my sister from me when she was only a baby and He gave me a life filled with foster homes and the dangers of the streets."

Belinda reached for Ruby's hand again and this time held it while she spoke.

"You look perfectly healthy to me and the fact that you are my neighbour shows me that you are living pretty well. You are still here, my dear, living and breathing. God must have known you have a purpose to keep you here on this earth. It's not how we start that determines our worth, it is how we finish and you, my dear, have a promising future."

Ruby was shocked by Belinda's response. She expected this sweet older lady to be shocked and appalled by her confessions. Instead, she made them sound like a blessing.

"We don't have all the answers for some of the tragedies we face in life. When I lost my beloved husband to cancer, my faith in God faltered for a long time. I was angry with God for taking away the love of my life because I had prayed so long for his complete recovery and felt God let me down. After my long commitment to Him, I felt He owed me a favour. When I finally came around and turned to Him for comfort, my life changed. I do not know why my dear husband left to be with the Lord but I am sure God knew he was something special. Since then, I travel with a small missionary group telling others about our Father and his love. It was always my dream to share His love with others. Now, I'm getting to share Him with you and feel blessed and honoured to do so. I can tell you are a lovely child."

Ruby was so overcome with the love she felt from Belinda. Belinda must have felt something too because she got up and embraced Ruby, who was still in her seat.

"Don't let the enemy lie to you one more day, sweetie. Take charge of life and walk in the love God promised for us all. You are beautifully and wonderfully made."

She squeezed Ruby tight and Ruby wrapped her arms around the woman's waist to return the hug.

Approximately two hours later, after sharing childhood stories with Belinda, who was kind and patient as Ruby rehashed her past and expressed her sorrow over her grandmother's and sister's deaths, and watching an interesting Christian program on television, Ruby thanked her new friend for her kindness and said her goodbyes. She was reluctant to leave but knew that Joe would be worried about her since she had left her cell phone behind.

Before she left, Belinda took Ruby's hand one more time.

"I have decided that I am going to adopt you as my granddaughter because you are such a lovely child and I truly enjoy your company," she said.

She walked over to her glass case, opened it, lifted the porcelain doll off the shelving and carefully handed it to Ruby.

"I want you to take Chantale and keep her as a token of our new friendship."

Ruby could not believe it. She had never met anyone who was so kind within only a few hours of meeting someone. Belinda's words and gestures made her choke up.

"I can't accept this, Belinda. Chantale spoke to you in the store," she said

"Oh pish posh," Belinda said. "Dolls don't speak, that was me just being silly. I really want you to take her and give her a good home. It would make me so happy!"

Ruby hugged Belinda with all her might while cradling Chantale in her arms.

"What can I do to repay all this kindness, Belinda? You have been way too nice to me," she said as she wiped a tear off her cheek.

"Well, since you ask, there is something you can do for me. I am going to visit a church that I have heard so much about and would love it if you would accompany me to service this Sunday!" she said with a mischievous smile on her face.

Ruby knew this was a setup but was delighted by Belinda's efforts.

"I'll come," she said. "Do you mind if I invite my fiancé as well?"

"The more the merrier, my dear child," Belinda replied with a smile.

"It's a date then!" she said and reached over to hug Belinda again with her free arm.

She practically skipped to her apartment and a realization came over her as she unlocked and then closed the door behind her. She asked God to give her a sign and he did, in the flesh. He sent her a living, breathing, walking, talking angel! He truly was real and truly did love her.

Ruby located her cell phone and saw that Joe had called her several times. She quickly dialed his number.

"Oh my goodness, baby, is everything alright?" Joe's concerned voice answered. "I was worried sick about you!"

"Joe, I'm good. No, actually, I am amazing! I have so much to tell you but I need you to come over right away." she said.

"Okay, sweetie, I'm on my way," Joe replied.

She ended the call, eager to tell Joe about her amazing encounter with Belinda. She could hardly contain the excitement and warmth that was brewing in her body. It reminded her of the tea she had at Belinda's and on a whim; Ruby picked up the phone again and redialed Joe.

"Hi, baby, everything okay? I'm on my way," Joe said instantly sounding worried.

"Do me a favour, babe? Can you stop at a store and pick up tea? I think it's called green tea. I would really appreciate it," she said.

"Tea? You don't drink tea," came the clearly confused reply.

"Oh, Joe, I do now! Things are different. I would really appreciate it!" she said with a grin.

"Will do, sweetie. Anything for my baby," Joe replied.

"And, Joe? I love you with all my heart and soul."

"Baby, are you sure everything is okay? I love you too."

"Trust me, Joe, everything is perfect. See you soon, bye."

Ruby placed Chantale safely on the dresser in her room and decided that she was going to get a glass case like Belinda's to start collecting dolls as well. She sat on her bed and closed her eyes. She needed to take care of something right away.

"Dear God. I am sorry about the things I said earlier and I thank you for always taking care of me. Please tell grandma I am going to be okay now, and tell my baby sister I miss her and I will always love her and I'll never forget her. God, I know now that you love me and did not do anything to hurt me. And God, thanks for my new friend, Amen."

And with that, she planted the seed she needed to start her new life.

Thirty One † Brandon

"Have you seen my black tie with the red stripes? It's not on the tie rack and I'm wearing my red shirt today," Brandon bellowed down the stairs to Aaron, who was in the kitchen getting juice for Angel.

They were getting ready for church and Brandon liked to look as sharp as possible when he attended. It was not protocol but he made it a priority to present himself well.

Since he gave his life to the Lord, things had changed so drastically. Aaron and Angel were now officially his family, he left his job and started a small accounting firm, and attended church and Bible study on a regular basis.

"You left it in the study, sweetie. It's hanging on the closet doorknob," she called back, shaking her head with a smile.

Brandon was not sure how he managed before living with Aaron. There was nothing in the house that she could not find and most times knew its location without even having to look. She was always mindful of his needs and treated him so well. They laughed, played and now prayed together, which he felt was what kept their marriage argument-free. Sure, they had many disagreements but they never carried anything over to the next day.

Karl, who Brandon learned enjoyed life to the fullest and was not afraid to have a good time, had really become a close friend and a mentor to him. It quickly made Brandon realize the misconception people who did not know any better had of Christians as strictly *Bible-reading-church-attending* folks. Nothing could have been further from the truth. Brandon had actually never enjoyed life as much as he did now—hanging out with Karl and the other church guys at local bars and clubs, dancing, having the occasional drink and listening to music. He was more responsible, yes, but he was not dead. He loved to think of how King David danced in the streets in praise and worship. Dancing was one of Brandon's favourite things to do.

Another thing in which Brandon had found pleasure was helping others. He was not the type to go around preaching the gospel but he shared it by helping others by making himself available for volunteer projects. There was a satisfaction he could not describe when someone he helped smiled at him or thanked him. He also liked helping out behind the scenes at church. He was on the tear down team that took care of taking things down on stage and making sure the church was back to its original state when service was over. Meanwhile, his love of all things media came in handy when it was time to get behind the cameras to record the service, which was broadcast on a local Christian station. It only took his natural talent and a few media training classes offered by the church to get the hang of it.

"Baby, are you ready to go?" Aaron shouted up from the main floor. "Angel is getting restless!"

Angel squealed on cue to confirm what her mom said.

"I'm coming," Brandon said.

He descended the stairs to his beautiful girls waiting for him at the bottom. Aaron never ceased to amaze him with how beautiful she was. Her beauty seemed to grow every day that they were together. Today, she wore her black, straight-legged, fitted dress pants with a royal blue, sleeveless, empire waist shirt that was made from soft chiffon, and was adorned with a beautiful jewelry set that complimented the colour of her top. Her loose curls were piled on top of her head with a black satin headband. She did not try to hide her scar anymore. Her eyes were done heavily but she wore her lips nude with a slight shine from her lip-gloss. His darling Angel was dressed in a frilly lavender dress that came to her knees and the cutest little ballet flats. Her curls, which were not as tight as before because her hair had grown a few inches, were tamed into a ponytail that now fell past her shoulders. He absolutely adored his little girl.

"Daddy, come!" Angel said.

Angel clearly made up for what Aaron lacked in bossy diva characteristics. She knew Brandon's heart was hers and used it to her advantage.

"Come to daddy, my little princess," he said.

He reached for her, smothering her with kisses before throwing her in the air. She giggled loudly and drooled on him in the process but he did not care. It was princess drool and that was special.

"Come on, daddy. Time to go," Aaron said giving him a loud kiss on the cheek. "We don't want to be late."

Brandon carried Angel out and strapped her into the car seat as Aaron locked up.

"Sweetie, you look so handsome today," Aaron said to Brandon, making him blush because no matter how many compliments she paid him, they always made him feel special.

"And you look stunning, my sweet!" he replied.

Brandon was excited about today's service, as Belinda Drummer, a travelling missionary, would be a special guest. Her story was one that deserved particular attention. Having lived in Alberta with her husband, doing good works in the western provinces of Canada, it was no secret that she went into isolation upon his passing. She then resurfaced with a new purpose in life, moving from province to province with a missionary group, which stayed in one place for a year or two, spreading the good news of Jesus Christ. The group of women was known as modern day Mother Teresa.

"I hope I get to meet Belinda Drummer today," he told Aaron. "I read her autobiography and fell in love with her giving spirit. She is the cutest little woman."

She enthusiastically agreed, having read bits and pieces of her story as well.

"Baby," Brandon cooed, "I love you."

"I love you too," she replied with a radiant smile.

He never got enough of hearing his beloved wife, Mrs. Aaron Conrad, say these words.

"Oh man, wipe that silly grin off your face," she teased catching him in one of his moments.

He stuck his tongue out at her and she playfully pinched his leg.

They pulled into the parking lot and it quickly became evident that a lot of people were coming to see the infamous Belinda Drummer and they had arrived earlier than usual. Brandon was thankful for the second row seats that Karl always saved for them. They hurriedly brought Angel to the baby centre, and joined Karl and his family.

Brandon eagerly scanned the front row, where all special guests sat with the pastor and the church team. Not spotting Belinda, he leaned over to Karl.

"Please tell me Belinda is going to be here."

"Oh, she's already here. She will be coming in with the pastor. The turnout to see her is so large that they thought it would be best if she was protected by the safety team and entered when the pastor does," Karl said.

"Well, I'm relieved to hear she is here," Brandon replied.

The praise and worship team stepped onto the stage, and the leader asked the congregation to rise and join them in song. Brandon and Aaron promptly fell into step with the beat of the familiar song. They both loved to dance, and often went to the altar to dance and worship unto the Lord. After a few fast-paced songs, the tempo slowed and the swaying bodies did as well. The pastor was brought in with her team and special guests. Brandon smiled as he recognized the little Italian woman who walked beside the pastor as Belinda Drummer. He did not, however, recognize the young woman and man who accompanied them but figured they must be Belinda's family.

"Isn't she adorable?" he asked Aaron who had a weird look on her face.

"She certainly is. Hey, doesn't that guy look familiar?"

"No, not really," he said, trying to get a view of the man whose features he could not make out as he was standing with his back to the second row.

As Aaron and Brandon fell back into the harmony of the worship song, Brandon found it hard to focus because of Belinda's captivating presence. But this was his time to show God how thankful he was so he forced himself to concentrate. When the song ended, the pastor made her way up on stage and delivered an extraordinary message. Soon, it was time to honour the special guest. After a short video of Belinda's travels, she was called up to the stage. There was something so special about this woman and Brandon hung on her every word about being blessed to bless others and giving all you can. He was determined to speak with her and get her to sign his book after service ended. Leaning over, he asked Karl whether he could make it happen and his friend promised he would try his best.

As soon as the service was over, and the pastor, her team and special guests were escorted out, Brandon grabbed Aaron by her hand and followed Karl to the back office.

Having managed to get into the private area, Brandon was shocked to see all the people who filled the room. Everyone was as excited as him to meet Belinda, who was shaking hands and exchanging cheek kisses with everyone who met her. When Brandon got closer, he pulled Aaron by the hand in the direction of where Belinda was sitting. He felt like an eager fan but was not ashamed.

As he was about to step forward to speak to Belinda, Brandon felt Aaron's body stiffen up. Brandon pulled her a bit harder but she seemed to be planted to the ground. When he turned to face her and see what the problem was, Aaron looked like she had seen a ghost.

"What's wrong, baby?" Brandon asked, instantly concerned for her well-being.

"I knew that guy looked familiar," she whispered. "That's Joe and there's Ruby."

Brandon could tell by her tone that she was on the verge of panicking.

"Ruby?" he asked. "Your old friend Ruby?"

"In the flesh," Aaron said as she nodded in her direction.

Brandon followed her gaze to a very pretty young woman sitting beside Belinda. Sure, she resembled Ruby but he remembered her to be butch-like with shortly cropped hair. This woman was lean with hair past her shoulders and looked very feminine. To make matters even more confusing, she was in a church.

"Are you okay?" Brandon asked Aaron.

He hoped and prayed that seeing Ruby would not stir up those awful memories of being gang raped. Although Aaron had moved past it, it still happened.

"Not really, babe. What on earth is she doing here?" Aaron's voice was shaky.

Ruby looked in Aaron's direction and made eye contact before Aaron could turn away. Before Aaron or Brandon could make a decision, she was headed in their direction. Brandon felt Aaron's body grow literally as stiff as a corpse.

"Aaron, is that you?" Ruby asked as she walked up to the couple. "Scar?"

Brandon cringed at the awful nickname that was no longer used in his world. Aaron stepped back and he stepped protectively in front of her.

"Hi, Ruby," Brandon said in a cold *I-am-only-being-friendly-because-I-have-no-choice* tone. "What can we do for you?"

He spoke on behalf of his wife, whom he knew was not in a good place right now. He could actually feel her body trembling.

"Um, I really don't know. I never expected to see you both...here. I guess I just want to let Aaron know that I am sorry for everything that happened to her and to us," she said to Brandon and then turned to face Aaron. "Aaron, I'm so sorry. I mean it.

I have changed. You have to forgive me."

Having watched the entire exchange, Joe came up and stood protectively behind Ruby. He must have known that she needed him.

Aaron said nothing and Brandon knew he had to take the lead.

"Ruby, now is not the time and this is not the place. We are here to see Belinda and that is all. I don't think my wife has anything to say to you right now and I would appreciate it if you backed off," he said.

"Your...wife? Oh my gosh, I'm so happy for you both!" Ruby exclaimed, refusing to leave them alone. "Aaron, you have to believe me. I've changed. I am engaged to Joe now and I have so much to tell you. Please listen to me."

Her pleading was becoming so frantic that it made Belinda turn her attention to the group and make her way over. Brandon could not believe how bad the timing was.

"Hello, my children," Belinda said, looking at each of the four emotional faces. "Ruby, please introduce me to your friends."

Ruby cleared her throat. "Belinda, this is Sc...I mean Brandon and this is Aaron—the same Aaron I told you about," Ruby said.

Belinda turned, facing Brandon and Aaron.

"Well now, don't we serve a mighty and powerful God? Isn't it wonderful how He reunites old friends?" Belinda said.

Her statement made Aaron find her voice and speak up.

"No disrespect to you, Belinda, but we are definitely not friends. In fact, I cannot stand this girl. She tried to ruin my life."

All former thoughts of forgiving Ruby seemed to leave Aaron's mind. Brandon spun around to try to calm her down, not wanting Aaron to lose her cool and say the wrong things in the presence of someone like Belinda. He regretted asking Karl to bring them to meet the missionary.

"My dear, I know the whole story. My darling granddaughter told me everything that happened. The good Lord taught us to forgive. Jesus forgave Judas for betraying him so we should always forgive each other. Let me finish off here and we shall all go to a quiet place and talk."

Without waiting for a response, she walked over to the pastor to bid her farewell.

Everyone stood in silence and an awkward tension filled the room. Aaron pulled Brandon to the side and whispered in his ear.

"I can't do this, Brandon. I'm going to freak out right now. I don't want to forgive her right now. I'm not ready yet."

"I know, sweetie, I know," he said soothingly rubbing her arms.

"Let's just get Angel and leave, right now," she said and rested her forehead on his chest.

Brandon wished he could erase her painful memories and heal her completely. She had been doing so well for so long and he worried about a relapse.

"Sweetie, we cannot just walk out without at least telling Belinda we need to go. I know you are hurt and you have a right to be but we cannot forget who we are right now. I'm here and won't let anyone harm you again."

Brandon glanced up at Ruby and Joe, and could see that this situation was just as hard for them. He was curious as to how these changes occurred for Ruby. If he correctly remembered Aaron's stories, she had no family. How had she become Belinda's granddaughter?

When Belinda came back over, she advised them that they could talk in one of the church's other private offices. Thankfully, Aaron agreed and soon they were all settled in a room with the two couples sitting on opposite sides of a boardroom table and Belinda sitting at the head. Belinda started by saying a prayer. Brandon could tell she was going to keep Jesus at the centre of this meeting.

"It is quite obvious that a lot of changes have taken place since you last saw each other. I have only known Ruby for a short period of time but I can assure you, God has really given her favour and is doing wonderful works in her life," Belinda said.

Aaron leaned forward, with her eyes focused on Belinda.

"I'm happy to hear that Ruby has made changes in her life. But to be frank with you, I question her motives. I have given Ruby a chance before and almost ended up dead! The night when I was..." she turned and glanced at Ruby for a second before focusing her attention back on Belinda, "*gang raped*, I lost my security, my pride and I almost lost my life with Brandon. We can't just act like what was done caused minimal damage. It was huge and truthfully," Aaron faced Ruby again, looking her straight in the eyes, "Ruby should be in prison for what she did to me!"

Brandon reached for Aaron's hand and squeezed it to let her know she had his total support.

Ruby spoke up.

"Aaron, what I did was horrific. Even now I cannot believe that I would ever do something like that, but I am not that person anymore. I was selfish and hated the fact that I was losing you. I hated the world and felt like everything in life was unfair. I know there is nothing I can say to change what happened but I really want you to know how sorry I am."

Tears started to flow from Ruby's eyes, and Joe handed her the handkerchief from his suit and held her hand.

"Aaron," Joe said, evidently feeling the need to speak on behalf of his fiancé, "Ruby is a changed person. I am a witness to how different she is now. We are engaged and Ruby gave up the street life. She is not the only one who changed. You have changed also. If anyone can understand how hard that is, it should be you." He protectively placed his hand on Ruby's back and gently rubbed it.

"I understand that the emotions stirring up within everyone come from a place of pain and fear," Belinda said. "When I lost my husband, I experienced these same feelings. What I learned was the enemy takes personal glory in knowing that these emotions exist and he feeds them. As children of the most high, we need to focus on the good things we are given in life and move forward. Aaron, your life is a testimony to the good grace of God. I can see you have a husband who loves you, and you found a church where the fellowship is rewarding and full of love. To move forward, you have to forgive and give to God anything that is too much for you. He doesn't give anyone more than they can bear."

"So, basically, you are telling me I should pretend nothing happened to me? I should just make believe that someone who I trusted with my life did not have me savagely raped like a piece of meat because she was mad at me and felt sorry for herself? I should just welcome her back into my life with open arms and believe that she wants the best for me?" Aaron shouted, with tears streaming down her face as the floodgates of emotions reopened. "Well, guess what? I can't do that. I will not do that! Ruby knew I had a child. She was there throughout my pregnancy and even helped me raise my daughter. She knew what was at stake and she did not care. Why should I care more for her than she did for me? Why?"

"Because the Bible says to forgive. I didn't say to forget. We have to move forward with wisdom in our lives, but you cannot carry the burden of what happened to you for the rest of your life. It will eat you alive and devour all the blessings God has in store for you. I know that is not easy to understand right now and I do not expect you to forgive right now, but I am asking you to pray about it and let the Holy Spirit guide you to a place of forgiveness. Both you and Ruby need to be released so you can move on with your lives," Belinda said.

Brandon appreciated Belinda's words. She was not trying to force Aaron to forgive Ruby by her own strength. That would be unfair. Even he had a big problem letting go of what happened to Aaron because he, too, had suffered because of it. He also knew what happened to Aaron was a very delicate topic that was never addressed between them and they had simply moved forward. But it was bound to surface one day and he knew it needed to be dealt with.

"I would like to say something," Brandon said, smiling at Belinda and then looking at Ruby and Joe. "What happened to Aaron was one of the most painful things I have ever experienced in my life, and the fact that I didn't protect her and I couldn't comfort her was rock bottom for me. We all suffered from it and, Ruby, I know you suffered as well."

He turned and faced his wife.

"Baby, I will never, ever minimize what happened to you. I can only imagine how you felt but no one here can truly understand the pain you suffered. All I can say is through your pain and suffering, we all found Jesus—even Ruby! Out of the darkness came a light that shone so bright it touched all of us. Our life together has changed so much now that Jesus is the centre of our relationship. I have never felt as satisfied and happy about my life as I do now. Nothing has given me more joy and peace than having you and Angel back in my life. You are a gift, one that Ruby lost. It is sad to say but her loss was my gain. However, as children of God, we must wish her the same blessings we want for ourselves and for the people we love. We, as a family, need to release Ruby and allow God to take over. If not, we are telling God that we only trust Him with part of our lives and I know that isn't true. We have to have faith in Him and trust Him, even when we do not feel like it. Baby, we have to walk by faith and not by sight."

Brandon pulled Aaron closer and wrapped his arms around her. She sobbed openly and there was not a dry eye in the room. When she calmed down, Aaron took a deep breath, turned, and faced Belinda.

"I want to forgive Ruby. No, I need to forgive her. Please tell me how to do this," she said.

"I can't tell you how to do it but I can lead you on the right path. Let's all join hands and pray. While we pray, I want everyone to have faith that the Holy Spirit will intercede on our behalf."

Belinda proceeded to pray so fervently that Brandon could feel the power of the Holy Ghost moving within the room.

For someone who was not there during the ordeal, Belinda prayed as though she was present all along. She touched on things that Brandon knew were brewing in the hearts of all the victims, including Ruby. She asked God for things they needed and to give them the tools to move forward. She called each name in the room individually, and asked God to rise up both him and Joe as strong pillars for the beautiful women with whom He had blessed them. She prayed for their futures, for a deeper relationship with God and fellowship with humanity. She prayed that they would all see that the battle was not theirs alone and that there was spiritual warfare on the earth for the children of God. Belinda closed by asking that they all find it in their hearts to forgive each other of their trespasses so God could forgive each and every one of their own trespasses against him.

When she was finished, she wrapped Aaron in her arms and told her everything was going to be okay. She kissed Aaron as if she was a child birthed from her own womb and Brandon's admiration for this stranger grew even more. She then hugged everyone else and told them all she loved them.

When Aaron looked at Brandon, he could see her spirit moving on a completely new level. There was a peace behind her eyes that he had never seen before and he was grateful. God never ceased to amaze him with the things He made possible. His wife then got up, walked over to Ruby and held her arms open while Ruby stepped in for the hug. Brandon was surprised but so proud that Aaron became the comforter. Ruby cried and instinctively Brandon knew they were tears of joy. He stood up, shook Joe's hand and told him to take care of Ruby. Joe nodded in agreement with a grateful smile on his face.

When it came time to collect Angel and leave, no promises were made to have further contact but Brandon knew that someday the couples would cross paths again. God was on time and in charge, and would bring them together when the time was right.

As they drove home in an appreciative silence, Brandon thought about his desire to meet with Belinda. He never imagined that she would help bring light to the darkness that had loomed within their hearts and lives. He knew his wife was totally free. Oh, yes, she was free indeed!

Thirty Two † Aaron

Finally, it is summer again and the weather is absolutely perfect. I have learned to enjoy even the little things and take the time to appreciate all that life has to offer. I love hearing the birds sing, and discovering new colours in all the natural things God provides, like leaves, flowers, animals and people. I adore spending time with Brandon and Angel.

Angel is such a wonderful little girl and I have so much hope for her future. I believe she helped to save my life or at least gave me the desire to want change. All you need is a want in your life to make a difference. It is hard to believe that there was a time when I believed material things and fancy clothes were confirmation of a good life. I really thought that I could be a successful prostitute and provide everything Angel needed because I was only considering the monetary things. I am so grateful that God took a hold of my life and changed me.

Brandon and I are also wonderful. My business is successful and my schedule is flexible. I am able to be a wife, a mother and a successful interior decorator. I am a triple threat and by that, I am very humbled.

I do not hear the voice anymore, but it has been replaced by something more powerful. I feel the presence of the Holy Spirit in me. Every time I do something good, my insides feel good. I use my conscience to guide me because I trust that God speaks to me through it and I have never been wrong.

I know you are curious about my relationship with Ruby. After that meeting with Belinda, I was changed. I thought that I was okay before but I had just buried the pain instead of getting rid of it. Well, now it is gone. I cannot explain it but I know it. It is as though that day never happened.

Ruby and I do not have the type of friendship we had before, but we are both in the same family. Brandon and I attended her wedding but we did not go to the reception. I was so proud to see her walking down the aisle and she was a beautiful bride. She and Joe are lucky to have found each other. Angel did not forget Ruby, and their love and bond never fizzled. That is the beautiful thing about children: They do not hold grudges. I have learned to rebuild my love for Ruby using Angel's example.

Ruby attends a different church than Brandon and I, and Belinda continues to mentor her. It is amazing how Belinda has become the family Ruby lost and desperately needed. Ruby has even gone on a few missionary trips with Belinda and the stories she tells me are enough to make me feel grateful for my new life and how blessed I am. Ruby also helps prostitutes on the streets and ministers to them. They actually listen to her because her name is still famous on the streets, and relate because she does not sugar-coat anything she went through.

After our meeting, Ruby went to the police station and filled in the blanks on my case. She turned herself in, spent the night in jail and was released on bail. I went to court, dropped the charges and Ruby was not prosecuted. I could not believe she did that but she wanted to help me with my healing and felt it was the right thing to do. Just that simple act showed me how much she cared and how sorry she was. Joe was at her side through it all and I am so happy Ruby has him in her life. I wish them all the best!

Brandon is such an awesome husband. He works less but has never had to compromise his finances. God blesses him so abundantly and we are still able to continue enjoying the same lifestyle. We give a lot, too. Having been so blessed, it is only right that we share with our community.

I am not saying that life is always easy. We face new dilemmas on a regular basis and sometimes the things that we are up against seem impossible to conquer in the moment but we always manage to get through them with prayer and faith. There is also so much more I want to do with my life, like follow Ruby's lead and minister to teens on the street. I do not think I am fully equipped for that yet and am waiting on God to provide the strength and the tools to do so. I have not been back to the streets since I left and know that it something I need to do. I gave my testimony at church a few weeks ago and when I was done, I had so many young women come up to me and tell me I touched their hearts and helped to restore their faith in God. God used me to show others His love and I have no regrets.

Actually, I have one teeny thing I need to do to feel totally at peace with my new life. I have not sought out my parents yet but I will—one day.

I often dream about the day when I make it to heaven. I cannot wait for God to wrap me in his arms. I live my life with God first in my heart. I mess up a lot but I know God knows my heart, and forgives me when I fail and allows me to keep going. When you think about it, what better purpose is there on earth than storing up favour and blessings for that mighty day? I cannot wait to look up into His beautiful face and hear the loving words for which we all long to hear:

"Well done, my beloved child, well done."

✝

Here is a sneak peak from the second book in the *hooked for God* series.

A Ruby for God

It is funny. I can remember when I ran these streets. I prowled the area daily looking for prospects to join my team. I could spot the vulnerable, weak, pathetic and needy females a mile away. The younger I found them; the better. New runaways, abused or lost young women in dire need of a protector. I would swoop in and promise them safety and a brand new life if they came and worked for me. These girls were so naive that they ate up everything I said without question. I became wealthy off of their bodies. They sold it, I collected—simple. Some called it pimping but back then I called it my hustle.

Deep inside, I had a heart for these young women and for the most part treated them well; unless of course they stepped out of line and I had to put them back in their place.

I kept myself planted inside strong emotional walls. On the streets, you walked with your game face on or the snakes, snipers and maggots would eat you alive.

It took just one girl to turn my life upside down. I met her as a runaway, saved her life and then she ditched me when she made it on top. Although she was just one of many, I could not let her go. But in pursuit of her, I found me and somebody very special.

Now I trudge these filthy streets in search of new prospects. Thank goodness I can still spot the vulnerable, weak and pathetic females from a mile away—it makes my new job easier. But instead of finding them to turn them into prostitutes, I am trying to save them and offer them a better life; a life off of the streets of hell and into the kingdom of heaven.

Oh yeah, by the way, my name is Ruby.

TASHA LEONA   302